Eleanor Gwynn
Cairo Egypt 1998-
99

Bandarshah

Bandarshah

TAYEB SALIH

Translated from the Arabic by

DENYS JOHNSON-DAVIES

KEGAN PAUL INTERNATIONAL
London and New York
UNESCO PUBLISHING
Paris

First published in 1996 by
Kegan Paul International
UK: P.O. Box 256, London WC1B 3SW, England
Tel: (0171) 580 5511 Fax: (0171) 436 0899
E-mail: books@keganpau.demon.co.uk
Internet: http://www.demon.co.uk/keganpaul/
USA: 562 West 113th Street, New York, NY 10025, USA
Tel: (212) 666 1000 Fax: (212) 316 3100

Distributed by

John Wiley & Sons Ltd
Southern Cross Trading Estate
1 Oldlands Way, Bognor Regis
West Sussex, PO22 9SA, England
Tel: (01243) 779 777 Fax: (01243) 820 250

Columbia University Press
562 West 113th Street
New York, NY 10026, USA
tel: (212) 666 1000 Fax: (212) 316 3100

UNESCO COLLECTION OF REPRESENTATIVE WORKS
Original titles: Volume I: *Dau al-Beit*
Volume II: *Meryoud*

© Tayeb Salih, 1968 and 1976, for the original text
© UNESCO 1996, for the English translation and notes

KEGAN PAUL INTERNATIONAL ISBN 0–7103–0537–0
UNESCO ISBN 92–3–103174–0

Phototypeset in Bembo by Intype London Ltd
Printed in Great Britain by
T. J. Press (Padstow) Ltd.

British Library Cataloguing in Publication Data

Salih, al-Tayyib
Bandarshah. – (Unesco Collection of Representative Works)
I. Title   II. Johnson-Davies, Denys   III. Series
892.736 [F]

ISBN 0 7103 0537 0

US Library of Congress Cataloging-in-Publication Data

Sālih, al-Tayyib
[Bandar Shāh. English]
Bandarshah / Tayeb Salih; translated from the Arabic by Denys
Johnson-Davies.
p.   cm.—(UNESCO collection of representative works)
ISBN 0–7103–0537–0
I. Johnson-Davies, Denys.   II. Title.   III. Series
PJ7862.A564B313   1996
892′.736—dc20   95–43489
                                                                 CIP

To the memory of my father

CONTENTS

FOREWORD

SEARCHING for an allegory about man, I found that he is like someone who has escaped from the danger of an enraged elephant into a well. He is suspended in it and has clung on to two branches that are at its opening to the sky. His feet have dropped down on to something in the wall of the well where four snakes have put out their heads from their holes. Then he looks down and sees in the bottom of the well a dragon with open mouth waiting for him to fall so that it may seize him. Raising his eyes to the two branches, he finds there two rats, a black one and a white one, gnawing away relentlessly and untiringly at them. While considering how best to deal with his situation, he sees close by him a beehive in which there is some honey. He tastes the honey and is so taken by its sweetness that his enjoyment prevents him from giving any thought at all to his predicament and from searching for an escape for himself. He does not bring to mind that his legs are above four snakes and that he does not know when he will drop on to them; he also does not bring to mind that the two rats are relentlessly cutting the branches and that once severed he will fall on to the dragon. He remains oblivious and heedless, captivated by that sweetness, until, falling into the dragon's mouth, he perishes.

I have likened the world, filled with banes, evils, perils and blights to the well. I have likened the four humours that are in the body to the four snakes; thus, when their components are aroused, it is like snake-bites, lethal poison. I have likened fate, from which there is no escape, to the dragon. To honey I have likened this little sweetness that man receives, tasting and hearing and smelling and touching and busying himself with, making him oblivious of his predicament and diverting him from the path of his goal. At this I became content with my lot and with improving what I could of my endeavours that perchance I might encounter, during the remainder of my days, a time when I would attain a guide to put me on the path, and control over myself, and meaning to my existence. I have abided in this state and have transcribed many books, and I departed from the lands of India having copied out this book.

KALILA WA DIMNA
from the chapter of *Barzawaih the Physician*

BOOK ONE

DAU AL-BEIT

CHAPTER ONE

MAHJOUB was like an old tiger, seated as in former times, despite the years and ill health, as though ever ready to spring: his hands on his stick and his chin on his hands, with his gown wrapped round his head and over his turban. The furrows in his cheeks had dug deep at the mouth, and on the forehead; that sharpness in the eyes had changed, with the passing of the days and with the memories of battles – and defeats no doubt – into a sick redness. In the eyes there was nothing but anger. We were in front of Sa'eed's shop, with the night speedily advancing on Wad Hamid. Addressing the sand at the spot where his stick was implanted in it, he said, 'You've been a long time away from the village.'

I lowered my head in thought. What could I say in such circumstances? Yes, it had been several years.

'Movement and being at rest are in God's hands,' I said to Mahjoub.

Taher Wad Rawwasi laughed in the way he used to laugh in the old days. From where he was sitting in the dark patch of sand, out of reach of the light of the lamp, he said, 'What would he do in this wretched village? He's better off in the place where he is.'

Abdul Hafeez had previously been the most tolerant of them, in the days when he had been able to look at things from both sides. But now, having defined his position, there was nothing strange about his saying in a quarrelsome voice devoid of affection,

'And where is his place? His place is here. However long or short a time he's away, his place his right here.'

'In any case,' I said, trying in vain to bring back time to what it had been, 'whether here or there, there's no more left to life than a matter of days.'

As though hearing the appeal for help, Wad Rawwasi said,

'Well, old friend, what should the likes of us say?'

Mahjoub continued to rest his hands on his stick and his chin on his hands.

Hamad Wad Rayyes wasn't there,[1] nor was Ahmed Abu 'l-Banat. Sa'eed stayed on in his shop, emptying things from boxes and putting them on shelves, aided by one of his grandsons. From deep inside the shop Sa'eed said something that Taher Wad Rawwasi understood and laughed at, while the night gathered up its coat-tails and, thickening, erased the landmarks of the village as one would erase chalk writing from a blackboard.

Suddenly I became aware of the muezzin's voice: 'Come to prayer. Come to salvation.' It was a weak feeble voice that lacked resonance. I asked about it and Abdul Hafeez said, 'It's Sa'eed's.' Still I couldn't make out whose it was, so Mahjoub said scornfully, 'Sa'eed Asha 'l-Baytat',[2] to which Wad Rawwasi said, 'Tell him Sa'eed the Owl – what would he know of Asha 'l-Baytat?'

'Sa'eed the Owl has become Asha 'l-Baytat?' I said. Mahjoub laughed, though not as he used to in days gone by, and said, 'And there's plenty more you'll be hearing and seeing.'

At this point Sa'eed came out of his shop holding a packet of cigarettes. He offered them round and we all, except for Mahjoub, took one.

'Seeing that Abdul Kareen Wad Ahmed's become a mystic, and Zein's become one of the leading personalities, and Seif ad-Din's about to become a Member of Parliament, what's so strange about Sa'eed the Owl being known as Sa'eed Asha 'l-Baytat?'

'Wonders will never cease,' I said, to which Sa'eed, who had in former times been nicknamed 'the Jurist', added, 'You need many lessons before we'll be able to teach you about the new state of affairs in the village. Do you think Wad Hamid's the same Wad Hamid you used to know?'

No, I didn't think so, but I had not expected that Sa'eed the Owl would have become a muezzin.

'What's happened to Seif ad-Din?' I asked them. 'Has he lapsed in his faith again, or what?'

'Are you still in the days of Seif ad-Din?' said Sa'eed. 'Maybe more than six people have held the position of muezzin since Seif ad-Din. Now, my dear sir, we're in the reign of Sa'eed Asha 'l-Baytat.'

'Seif ad-Din deserted the Imam ages ago,' said Taher Rawwasi. 'He's become, you might say, an in-between – one foot in heaven and one in hell.'

'Like everyone nowadays,' said Sa'eed. 'In these times everyone's become an in-between.'

I heard Mahjoub grunting with rage like an infuriated camel, and Taher said, 'And you, Father of Laws? Have you become one of today's people or are you firmly set in your ways like the Tiger Mahjoub?'

Sa'eed fell silent, as though being reminded of his old nickname had taken him by surprise; then half laughing, half in anger, he said, 'May God bless the times when there were such things as laws. Now Bakri's boys call me Sa'eed the Troublemaker. Today anyone seeking his rights is dubbed a troublemaker.'

Mahjoub added in the same manner, 'Whatever Bakri's boys turn to, may God not make things right for them.'

I asked Mahjoub what Bakri's boys had been up to.

Abdul Hafeez had made his ablutions during this conversation without taking part in it, mumbling supplications to himself. When the final call to prayer was given in the mosque courtyard, he rose hurriedly, saying, 'Let's get to prayers otherwise we'll miss them.'

It was as though I were expecting something that wouldn't happen, for Mahjoub too stood up, leaning on his stick, sighing and groaning.

'I'd better go home,' he said. 'The night's getting on.'

'Have dinner with us,' Sa'eed called out behind them, 'even if it's only for the sake of the guest.'

Mahjoub went off as though he hadn't heard.

'Dinner can wait,' said Abdul Hafeez from afar, 'but community prayers won't.'

Taher Rawwasi came and sat alongside me on the bench. For a while we kept silent as I listened intently to the night sounds of Wad Hamid. The bleating of sheep, a cow or bull lowing, the sounds of a quarrel, snatches of singing from a radio; a jumble of screams meeting and parting at some place from some direction – you don't know whether they're sounds from a funeral or from a wedding, or whether they're from upstream or down. The headlights of a car approach, rise up and pass on. Water pumps on the river bank and the whispering of the cool night in the palm fronds; Sa'eed's shop as it has always been and the patch of sand as it has always been, and the night and the stars.

'Poor Mahjoub, he has aged,' said Taher Rawwasi.

'How is it, Rawwasi my boy,' said Sa'eed from deep inside the shop, 'that you don't age when you're older than all of us?'

'Because my heart's cold,' said Taher. 'People like you and Mahjoub have hearts full of fire. In these times one should stand aside and be an amazed spectator.'

Sa'eed came out and sat on the bench beside us.

'The whole world's grown old and this bench is just as it always was,' I said to Sa'eed.

Sa'eed laughed and said, 'That's the work of Wad Baseer, God's mercy be upon him. You'd think it was made of iron. Things today are made like cardboard.'

'For all his fieriness of heart Mahjoub's got asthma,' said Taher. 'He's had a rough time.'

'By God, brother,' said Sa'eed, 'we're all hanging on by the skin of our teeth. If it's not asthma it's a pain in the kidneys, the stomach or the joints. But God is merciful.'

'It's because you won't listen,' said Taher. 'Ages ago we used to tell you you should take fenugreek and ginger: ginger in the morning on an empty stomach, and fenugreek before going to sleep. And, if you really want to know what's what, you should also drink a glass of ghee every day.'

'We've tried it all and it hasn't worked,' said Sa'eed, 'home cures and foreign. Injections of penicillin and vitamins. We've drunk qarad and harjal juice and we've nibbled away at garlic and onions. And then there were those people who said smear yourself with henna and others who said have a good sweat over a talh fire. My friend, it all depends on the body's original state of health.'

'By God, you're right,' said Taher. 'There's nothing like activity. This body, what burdens we've made it bear. Ah, my friend, one was like a mule – one kick and you'd bring down a mountain.'

There reigned a silence that had the flavour of those days, days when Taher Rawwasi and his companions, the Mahjoub gang, would sit on that patch of sand in front of Sa'eed's shop, and Taher Rawwasi would give a deep sigh and say, 'Time comes and Time goes.'

Taher Rawwasi gave as deep a sigh as was possible for the lungs of a man who had passed seventy, and said, 'Where will we ever find such days again, Hajj Sa'eed.'

Sa'eed's grandsons had spread out the mats in front of the shop and placed a large tray on them. The three of us got up and seated ourselves by it. Hardly had Sa'eed raised the covering than Abdul Hafeez arrived. He seated himself between us, saying, 'Didn't I tell you that dinner could wait?'

'May your prayers be accepted, Hajj,' Sa'eed said to him.

'The Imam's ill today,' said Adbul Hafeez.

'Who led the prayers in his place?' said Taher.

'Taher's making out he doesn't know,' said Sa'eed. 'His deputy of course. When the Imam's not there, who else would lead the people in prayer?'

'The Imam's deputy must be you,' I said to Abdul Hafeez.

Sa'eed and Wad Rawwasi will never give up their silliness,' said Abdul Hafeez. 'There's no question of a leader and his deputy — when the Imam's not there anyone can lead the people in prayer.'

'Anyway,' said Taher, 'For some time now the Imam hasn't been so well. It's as if he hasn't been all that concerned about prayers. What do you think, Hajj Abdul Hafeez, about your being Imam and having done with it?'

'Listen,' Abdul Hafeez said angrily, 'you've become white-haired but you've got the minds of children. Do you imagine being an Imam is a joke? He's a man who's learned and well versed in religion. The whole district hasn't got an Imam like him. When God takes him to Him, then we shall see.'

'What are you so angry about?' said Sa'eed. 'Taher's right. Isn't the whole thing just a matter of the prayers for the two Feasts, the Friday sermon, and the special prayers in Ramadan?'

'Thanks be to God, Lord of the worlds, and not of those who are astray. Amen,'[3] added Wad Rawwasi. 'And even the Friday sermon is summed up in a couple of words: God grant victory to the Moslems and protect the Commander of the Faithful[4] — though what we'd like to know is, where is this Commander of the Faithful?'

'There is no strength or power except through God,' said Abdul Hafeez. 'And what, Wad Rawwasi, do you know about the Imam's sermons? You've never performed ablutions in your whole life. From the time God created you you haven't entered a mosque or even put a foot over the threshold.'

'Have a fear of God, Abdul Hafeez,' said Sa'eed. 'How can you saw Wad Rawwasi hasn't seen the inside of the mosque? Was there anyone who gave more help than he did in building the mosque?'

'Do you see, Meheimmed,' said Wad Rawwasi, directing his words at me, 'how people nowadays deny the truth? By God, Ibrahim Wad Taha was right. He used to say to me, "Wad Rawwasi, keep well away from people with beards and prayer-beads — you'll get nothing but trouble from them." In the heat and the cold, who was it who carried the water and the bricks? Who was it who worked on until the roof was put on? Who worked all night long when people were snoring in their beds? Who? But what's the use of going on about it?'

'Because of this sort of talk,' shouted Abdul Hafeez angrily, 'I've stopped sitting at Sa'eed's shop. I swear by Almighty God, if it weren't for this man who's our guest, I wouldn't have come to this gathering.' With a gesture of washing his hands of it all, he rose to his feet.

'Have you gone crazy or what?' Sa'eed shouted at him. 'It's all in fun. Do you want to prohibit people from talking? Brother, don't you see the mosque standing there? Is anyone wanting to buy it or sell it? Those who pray and those who don't, they all worked on it, and the wages and the reward are with God. In the name of God the Merciful, the Compassionate. Brother, do you want to start Islam off again right from the beginning?'

I told Abdul Hafeez not to be upset, but he didn't relent.

'You are people whose discernment has been blinded by our Lord,' he said. 'This kind of talk is neither here nor there — it's better not said. Peace be upon you.' And off he went.

CHAPTER TWO

I F THINGS appeared to me as I have recounted to you on that journey, then maybe it can be pleaded in my defence that I didn't mean to deceive you. My grandfather was as I told you, and my relationship with my grandfather used to appear to me at that time, and for long years afterwards, as I told you on that journey. Then there befell that catastrophe that defies description, be it in a single journey or in several, or even in a whole lifetime. Suddenly the harmony in the universe had been disrupted. And so, between night and morning, we found ourselves not knowing who we were or what our situation was in terms of time and place; on that day it appeared to us that what had happened had happened all of a sudden. Then, bit by bit, it was borne in upon us, while on that stormy ocean between doubt and certainty, that what had happened was like the falling in of the roof of a house: it doesn't just fall all at once but starts to fall from the time it is first put into place. Yes, we did resist in various ways. We said that what had happened was something unique, having no bearing on what had been or would be, an isolated phenomenon, as though a goat were to give birth to a calf or a date palm to produce oranges. Then we told ourselves that what had happened to Bandarshah and his sons was just such a phenomenon, but that it wouldn't happen to us because we weren't like Bandarshah and his sons. And people would answer one another, clinging to the flimsiest of reasons – you're right, you're right – and then falling into a brittle and troubled silence, just as someone in great pain quietens down for a moment, then the state of panic would return as one of them would say, 'Friends, have a fear of God. How can you say Bandarshah and his sons aren't like us? I swear they're like us and better than us. By God, they were the best of men.'

A deeply buried fear would seize hold of us because we knew that this was the truth. When Bandarshah used to attend a wedding or a funeral he would be surrounded by his eleven sons and his grandson Meryoud. All eyes would be raised to them, all thoughts concentrated on them because they glittered in people's eyes and were the pride of the village.

'Friends,' one of us would say enviously, 'it's as though the Night of Power[5] had been opened for Bandarshah. Wherever he puts his foot he finds benefit. The date crop this year is bad for everyone except for Bandarshah.'

At once, more than one voice is raised against the dissident: 'Ask pardon of God, are we also going to envy Bandarshah? Do you or we expend a quarter of the energy Bandarshah and his sons do?'

And the dissident would quickly reconsider things, saying, 'By God, you're right, friends. Bandarshah and his sons aren't like us. They're people our Lord is pleased with. Every bit of good that comes to them is well deserved.'

Our astonishment never ceased at the strange likeness there was between Bandarshah and his grandson, Meryoud, for the grandson, in appearance and behaviour was a complete replica of his grandfather, as though the Great Artificer had fashioned them at one and the same time from the same piece of clay, presenting Bandarshah to the people of the village, then, after fifty or sixty years, presenting Bandarshah once again to them in the form of Meryoud. Imagine twins, the birth of one preceding that of the other by fifty or sixty years. The build, the face, the voice, the laugh, the eyes, the brilliant whiteness of the teeth, the jutting jaw, the way they had of standing and sitting and walking. And when they shook you by the hand they would both apply their whole body to your hand, looking at you, not like other people do, face to face, but with a sideways glance, affectionate and yet probing and appraising. And when you stood between them, it was as though you were standing between two mirrors placed opposite each other, each reflecting the same image in an endless extension.

Meryoud was the grandfather's agent and deputy; the complete embodiment of his authority. I remember being greatly astonished the first time I saw that. Meryoud was a year or so older than me and at that time was no more than fifteen. He came to my grandfather in the forenoon when my grandfather had with him Mukhtar Wad Hasab ar-Rasoul, Hamad Wad Haleema and myself. As usual I was tucked away in a corner, only speaking when I was asked something and then doing so with no more than a sentence or two. Meryoud entered, greeting each merely by his name without saying Uncle So-and-so or Grandfather So-and-so, then sat down in front of my grandfather without being given permission to do so. No, he wasn't insolent, just possessed of a self-confidence that bordered on insolence. Wasting no time on formalities, he went straight to the point, ignoring the other two men: 'Bandarshah says he's bought the calf from you.'

'Bandarshah's free to buy or not to buy,' said my grandfather. 'I, though, haven't sold.'

'If Bandarshah has bought from you,' said Meryoud, laughing, 'then you must have sold.'

'Your grandfather offered twelve,' said my grandfather, 'and I'm asking seventeen.'

Saying nothing, Meryoud took from his pocket a roll of pound notes, which he handed to my grandfather, who took them without counting them, though he kept them for an instant in the palm of his hand as though weighing them, then said, 'The calf's tied up in the pen – go and take it.'

'I drove the calf off at daybreak,' said Meryoud, laughing, as he made to leave. 'Its meat is now cooking over the fire, maybe they've even eaten it.'

When he had left, I said to my grandfather, 'How much did he pay?'

'Twelve,' said my grandfather.

Taking the notes, I counted them and found that they were indeed twelve pounds.

As he took back the money from my hand, having noticed my astonishment, my grandfather said, 'The boy paid in cash. At any rate dealing with the boy is better than dealing with his grandfather.'

On that day my grandfather was happy at that abnormal event. I saw Mukhtar Wad Hasab ar-Rasoul's narrow eyes growing wider with unreserved reverence. Hamad Wad Haleema gazed at Meryoud, as he left guffawing with laughter, as a human created of clay might gaze at an angel that has descended from above. I won't conceal from you that all this left its impression on me. At that moment I felt that I had been witnessing a miracle. Had someone told me that day that the Fates had chosen Meryoud to effect a reconciliation between the past and the future, I would have believed it. My grandfather, despite his caution, had believed it, as had all the inhabitants of the village. Yet what a momentous thing occurred that forenoon. The winds were coming from far-away caverns shrieking blood and thunder; the afreets were leaping down from the roofs of houses and branches of trees, from the fields and sand-dunes and mountain passes, from under the hooves of cattle, from the bends of alleyways, wailing and howling and shrieking and screaming unintelligible words. Then the hubbub manifested itself in one single word: Bandarshah. Despite the great distance of time, I cannot now recall that forenoon without a shiver. It was as if the village had been torn out from its roots by some fearsome bird, which had then carried it in its claws, had circled around with it, and then cast it down from on high. I was like a person in the grip of a nightmare filled with screaming and movement, while he is paralysed amidst it all incapable of going forwards or backwards. It was as though chaos were exploding beneath our feet, while people ran helter-skelter here and there in search of something – and there was nothing; looking for the source – and there was no source. All the images were like specks of dust that no sooner settled in the mind than they disintegrated into fragments – and with them the universe and life. It was thus that I saw Hamad Wad Haleema that day, moving forward, then retreating, as though asleep or dead, the plaything of powers unseen.

On the fringes of that nightmare, bareheaded women, their faces covered in dust, were grasping at men whose hands were fettered and tied with a thick rope to a camel's saddle; on the camel a shoulder carrying a gun, with tens of men barring his way. Then, with a rushing and a roaring, the images are welded together, mingle and form a tangible shape, that of Bandarshah in the form of Meryoud; or Meryoud in the form of Bandarshah; and it is as though he is sitting on the throne of that hubbub, gripping the threads of chaos in both hands, amidst it and above it at one and the same time, like a resplendent and destructive ray.

We were like a vast flock of frightened birds, meeting and parting, rising and falling, circling round each other, making a horrible screaming sound that deafened the ears. On that forenoon the past and the future were murdered and no one was there to bury their corpses or mourn them.

Yes, our neighbour Masood had a beautiful voice and a serene laugh that resembled something sweet and delightful, and which on that day I imagined to be the sound of gurgling water. It had been the date harvest, as was told in that story,[6] and its transportation by camel and donkey, and the business of my grandfather with our neighbour Masood, and of me with my grandfather. Probably the place where that incident occurred would have remained clear and distinct from the other incidents of my life – had it not been that we had got up one morning to find that suddenly we were certain of nothing.

CHAPTER THREE

'They say you are now called Sa'eed Asha 'l-Baytat,' I said to Sa'eed, who had previously been nicknamed Sa'eed the Owl.

He gave his innocent laugh, which I remembered from the days of my childhood in Wad Hamid, and said in his bedouin accent.

'The woman Fattouma, God spare you, when the arak's gone to her head, talks all sorts of rubbish.'

'And you mean to say that Fattouma sang at your wedding?'

'O Meheimeed, brother,' he said, 'in these days money doesn't just produce Fattouma – I'm telling you, money brings along the very air itself by its horns.'

'What did Fattouma say about you?' I asked.

Proudly twirling his small moustache that sat uneasily over his lips, as did the excessively large turban on his head, he said, 'Fattouma, the devil take her – don't think it was just ordinary singing. A wedding at which Fattouma doesn't sing can't really be called a wedding.'

I repeated the question to him and he said, 'I'm telling you, yours truly had a wedding that made the people of the village forget Zein's wedding.[7] Ask anyone you like and he'll tell you there hasn't been a wedding like Sa'eed's.'

Zein's wedding had been a wonder. That Sa'eed the Owl, though, should become the son-in-law of the Headmaster, with his lofty social standing, was nothing short of a miracle.

'God keep you safe,' said Sa'eed. 'We didn't know where to find room for all the people. Tribe upon tribe they were. Every tribe was one to be reckoned with. We made the marriage contract in the mosque. The Imam said to the men, "Every one of you look and listen: Sa'eed's a man in a million – no one should say Sa'eed' the Owl." '

I was longing to know what Fattouma had said. I repeated the question, and he said, 'Fattouma, the devil take her – she describes things so aptly you'd think she was reading from a book. She certainly earned her ten pounds.'

'My! My! Ten pounds?'

'Ten whole pounds, upon my honour, Meheimeed. I said to her, "Now listen here, woman, the proverb says: Give to the singer and see him on his way, but give to the maddah[8] and dine him. I want a name from you, one that will make the people of Wad Hamid forget for evermore the nickname Sa'eed the Owl." God bless you, they really drove me crazy with the *Owl, the Owl*. God curse them. She said to me, "When the circle's full of people and the dancing's at its height, you'll see what sort of song Fattouma will produce." '

'And then, Sa'eed – how did Fattouma describe you?'

'God keep you safe, when things were at their climax, she rose and the girls let down their hair – like this – and entered the circle. Yours truly was standing like Antar[9] brandishing the whip. God bless you, Fattouma.'

'Yes – and then?'

'She said a lot of things. Ask Ahmed Abu 'l-Banat about them. He remembers them all, God bless him. Just listen to these words:

> "When Thursday last the news did come to me
> I let out cries of joy and poured out praise
> To you, O man of chivalry.
> I admire you, O Sa'eed, O Asha 'l-Baytat."

And how about this:

> "Charming Sa'eed's the islands' crocodile.
> His fame has risen, has spread through towns.
> Asha 'l-Baytat, cavalier of the clans.
> Give trilling cries of joy, O girls –
> He's the bridegroom of the Headmaster's daughter." '

Here he was so overcome with delight that he stood, drumming with his feet and leaping about and waving his hand as though in a circle of dancers.

'But how did the Headmaster accept?' I said to him.

'He had no choice,' said Sa'eed immediately.

'How come?' I said.

He was silent for a while as though thinking, then said, 'Didn't

I serve him with my own hands? It was coming up to a thousand pounds. He wanted to cheat me of them.'

Sa'eed used to sell charcoal and firewood and work in the fields, and he would give the money he'd earned to the Headmaster for safekeeping.

'Friend,' I said to him, 'have a fear of God – where did you get a thousand pounds from?'

'If you don't believe me, ask the Imam,' he said. 'Ask Sheikh Ali and Hajj Abdul Samad.'

'You mean to say,' I said to him, 'that the Headmaster married you to his daughter in return for the money you'd saved with him?'

'You saw Sa'eed the Owl, Sa'eed the Dumb,' he said. 'God keep you safe, don't think I don't know him inside out. It's something I'd had carefully planned for ages.'

'How?' said I. 'Do you mean to say you'd had your eye on the Headmaster's daughter for a long time?'

'Good God, what do you think?' he said. 'You yourself know the work I used to do in the Headmaster's house: "Sa'eed, fill up the water jars; Sa'eed, bring fodder for the animals; Sa'eed, chop the firewood." Was all that for nothing?'

'God forbid – and then?'

'And then nothing. Maybe for over seven years I worked like a donkey. Whenever I had got together five piastres – or ten or twenty, or a pound – I'd go to my friend Abu 'l-Banat for him to mark it up for me in his account book, and then I'd go and give it to the Headmaster. Every year he'd say to me: "Sa'eed, why don't you come and take your money?" and I'd say to him "Keep it with you, it won't go away." Year after year and piastre on top of piastre. During this period his middle daughter got married and divorced. Ugly and short-sighted she is. I held myself in patience for two or three years, while the girl was just sitting about. There wasn't a soul who was after her. I said to myself, "Sa'eed, this is it. Matters have come to a head." '

Through sheer astonishment I interrupted him, 'The devil take you, you wicked fellow – all that and we were calling you dumb?'

He laughed and said, 'Friend, is anyone dumb? Man's too cunning, even for the jinn.'

'And then, you rogue?'

'And then I took up the account and hurried off to see the Headmaster. I knew he was in a bad way after he'd been put on pension and that he'd spent the money. I said to him, "By God, your Excellency, I am in need of the money." Oh, you should have seen him squirming and fidgeting. Then he said to me, "Come tomorrow. I haven't got the money in ready cash. To cut a long story short, I went back and forth and was told to come back tomorrow and after tomorrow. Then I said to him, "Listen, Excellency, you don't have any money, so let me make you a proposition: give me this short-sighted daughter of yours in marriage and we'll call it quits." He was sitting on a chair just as you're sitting now and it was in the afternoon. He gave a great leap from the chair. Yours truly got himself ready – I told myself we were going to come to blows. You know what an arrogant person His Lordship is. He said to me, "Are you out of your mind? Do you think there are no laws in the place? You, the dirty, stinking Sa'eed marrying my own daughter?" He thought he'd frighten me. I swear to you, yours truly stood his ground. I said to him: "Hey!" – after that there was no more Your Excellency – I said to him, "Hey – get an earful of this – I'm Sa'eed Wad Zayed Wad Hasab ar-Rasoul. I'm a free Arab. I swear to you, my people in Sodari are so numerous they'd blot out the sun's light. What's wrong with me? A Moslem who believes in the Oneness of God – and I, that dirty, stinking one, will be marrying your daughter. And your daughter isn't such a catch: ugly, half-blind and divorced. If she sat around till Doomsday, she'd not find anyone better than me. And if you still refuse, I give you my word, I'll take you in and out of court till I get my money from you." '

I pictured to myself the Headmaster, with his haughtiness and elegance of speech, in this humiliating situation with a man to whom he gave friendship as a sort of charity.

'And then, Sa'eed?'

Sa'eed crossed his legs and sipped from the cup of coffee in front of him. Then, with ludicrous and studied gracefulness, he put down the cup, while I prepared for him to hold centre stage of events in Wad Hamid for an hour or two, as though he had become in that moment the pole around which the universe revolves.

'I had already settled the matter with the good lady, the girl's mother, may God bless you, Fatima bint at-Taum. I swear she's a woman who's worth a whole tribe. I knew about her being related to ourselves – her mother's from our people, the Koz bedouin.'

'Fatima bint at-Taum's mother is from your people?'

17

'Yeah, why not?' Isn't Fatima bint at-Taum's mother Haleema bint Rabih? And the venerable Imam himself – you know where his mother is from?'

'Don't tell me she too is one of your people?'

'In the name of God the Merciful, the Compassionate – are you stupid or what, Meheimeed? The Imam's mother, Marha bint Jadeen, she and Haleem bint Rabih are first cousins.'

'Good Heavens! You mean you'd got things sewn up on both sides?'

'The Headmaster said "Never." When I found no other way I said to myself that there was no one but our Sheikh Haneen. I got up at night and went to the tomb. I said to him "O Sheikh of ours, I've come to ask something of you and I shall not leave empty-handed." I stayed on all night. I slept for a while, then I heard a noise. Opening my eyes, I found him standing there above my head. He said to me: "Go and make the call to prayer. Your request is granted." When I came down from the minaret after the call to prayer, the Imam said to me, "Sa'eed how did you know that Hamad was unwell today?" I said to him, "Never mind who told me." After the prayers the Headmaster, unbidden, said to me, "Sa'eed, that's it – the wedding will take place, God willing." May God keep you safe, I shouted out at the top of my voice, "O Sheikh Haneen, may you be blessed by God." I said this three times. The people said, "Has the man gone crazy or what?" Off I went and slaughtered an animal as a sacrifice. I told them that I wanted a real tip-top wedding, right from the start, with singing and dancing and the whole works and that we'd bring Fattouma. The Headmaster became like putty in my hands. I'd say to him right and he'd say right; I'd say to him left and he'd say left. God keep you safe, the wedding rocked the district, from the quarter of the Talha right up to the Koz bedouin. Alongside it Zein's wedding was like a circumcision ceremony. I tell you my friend, may God keep you safe, I didn't know myself – yours truly was strutting around in the Headmaster's courtyard. I waved my arms above Fattouma and put down a pound for her – that's apart from the ten she took in advance. It was then the good lady sang:

"Charming Sa'eed – how proud his mother must be!
Whatever he wants may the Lord make it be.
The people have gathered and he's married well;
O you who him envy, you'd better not tell."

'The trilling cries of joy rang out and my head was up on the ceiling with pride.'

'Fine,' I said, 'and how come you became the muezzin?'

'O, that's nothing,' said Sa'eed. 'I swear to you I did it out of charity, for the sake of Almighty God – and anyway Hamad said he was tired of climbing up the minaret every day.'

'Anyway, from the minute you became the Headmaster's son-in-law, the rest was child's play.'

'What's a Headmaster?' he said contemptuously. 'I don't give a damn about the Headmaster or even the Omda.[10] I've got money. I'm telling you, if this very day I wanted the Omda's daughter, I'd have her.'

'And where did the money come from?' I said to him. 'Or have you found yourself some treasure trove?'

He got to his feet, laughing happily, and said, 'I must go off to the souk – I'll tell you the story of the money another time.'

And he went off, humming to himself in his weak, feeble voice:

'Charming Sa'eed – how proud his mother must be!
Whatever he wants may the Lord make it be.'

CHAPTER FOUR

Hamad Wad Haleema recounts that one day, when they were still young lads, Isa Wad Dau al-Beit came out and joined them dressed up as for the Feast, though it was not the time of the Feast. He was wearing a new gelabia made of silk and had on his head a new embroidered red skullcap and pure white turban, while on his feet there shone a pair of red shoes. Hamad said that Isa's appearance was truly weird among lads some of whom were naked, while others wore nothing but a piece of old rag round their middles or were dressed in clothes that were tattered or filthy. 'He appeared to us both strange and ludicrous. When I first saw him I shouted, "Bandarshah", and we all began repeating, "Bandarshah, Bandarshah," and we chased after him till we made him go into his house. From that day no one called him anything but Bandarshah.'

'This business of names is extraordinary,' Hamad went on. 'Some people's names are just right for them, fitting them to the life. You have Hasan Timsah,[11] Allah Leena Wad Jabr ad-Dar,[12] Bekheit Abu 'l-Banat,[13] Suleiman Akal an-Nabag,[14] Abdul Mowla Wad Miftah al-Khazna,[15] Al-Kashif Wad Rahmatallah.[16] Every one of them has a name that fits him as a scabbard fits a sword. But you'll find the lot of them real terrors, may God protect you from their evil. I, for instance, people call me Wad Haleema,[17] no one uses Abdul Khalek. The reason? Ask Mukhtar Wad Hasab ar-Rasoul, whatever he turns to may God not make things right for him.'

Hamad gathered his gown round his thin frame and said, 'When we were boys we used to study the Koran in Hajj Saad's mosque. Mukhtar was a boy who was very pleased with himself, with bulging muscles and much feared. After the lessons, we would gather under the big sayyal tree, which is there to this very day. Mukhtar used to stand in the middle of the circle with bared back, taking his stand for the contest. Those were the days of valour and manliness and faint-hearted boys couldn't survive amongst those crocodiles. In what did the context consist? A whip as long as your arm made of the roots of the sant tree. God bless our Prophet, a boy wouldn't be able to stand more than a stroke or two at the most from Mukhtar Hasab ar-Rasoul. As for him, he had a back like a hippopotamus – however much you flogged him it made no impression. I myself couldn't take being whipped at all. I would stand far off, having nothing to do with it all, and let them all get on with it. The whole day Mukhtar would be standing there in the middle of the circle, and the boys would go in one by one. One stroke, two strokes, and out they'd come. One stroke, two strokes, next. Whenever Mukhtar met up with me he'd make fun of me, calling me by my mother's name because of the great contempt he had for me. He'd say to me, "Wad Haleema, when are you going to become a man and enter the circle with the other men?" The jibe would cut into my heart like a knife and I would become extremely annoyed. But I was small and puny. What was to be done? Then one day I took matters in hand: life or death, I didn't care – anything was better than being called Wad Haleema. I tell you, man's a tricky customer, the smallest thing can set him off – tread on his toes too hard and there's no knowing what he won't do. After lessons I ran home. I took a bag of red pepper, maybe a pound of it. I tucked it away on me and off I went high up into the wilds, till the houses seemed like mirages. Red pepper it was, like God's raging fire; I ate a lot of it, then stripped naked and rubbed some of it all over my body. God save you from the fire that broke out in my body. Hell-fire broke loose as I screamed out at the top of my voice: Aiy! Aiy! and it was all open wasteland and there was no one to hear as I hurled myself about and rolled in the dust. The sweat poured off me in torrents. O my friend, what pain there was, God bless those listening – something to really drive you out of your mind. After that I didn't care about a thing – I could go into the fire and not feel anything. I ran on, my shirt in my hand, my eyes shooting out sparks, my head swollen big as a water jar. I reached the sayyal tree where I found Mukhtar Wad Hasab ar-Rasoul, who was all too well known to me, standing there like Antar, having finished off the whole lot of them. Right away I went in and stopped in front of him and took up my stand. He looked at me with contempt. He said, "Wad Haleema, have you become a man today? Get along – I don't have contests with mother's boys." God is great. I glared at him with eyes like sparks. I said to him, "If you're a man, strike." He smiled and laughed, looking this way and that while the group laughed. By God, they were too hasty with their laughs. Wad Miftah al-Khazna and Wad Rahmatallah laughed particularly loudly. They said "Wad Haleema's got himself into real trouble." He took hold of the whip, bent it with both hands and flicked it in the air with resounding cracks. Then he walked around me, giving me light pecks with it here and there, hoping to shake me, but I'd got sixty thousand afreets in my head. Then he took up his stance, planting his right foot firmly on the ground, twirled the whip about and brought it down. I swear by your life, it felt cold and fine by me after the fire of the pepper. My skin was benumbed as though dead – if you'd stuck a knife into it I wouldn't have felt a thing. He gave me the second and third strokes, while I stood firm as a wall. If that door over there can feel, then I felt. When he came to the seventh stroke he stopped. He stepped back from me and regarded me with astonishment. I gave him such a venomous look he caught his breath. My friend had begun to be shaken. There was no longer any laughter – the people were as quiet as could be. The laughter of Wad Miftah al-Khazna and Wad Rahmatallah grew dry in their throats. May God keep you safe, I felt as though there were some giant ogre in my stomach, moving and blossoming and spreading its wings above the whole earth. I felt as though I were some gigantic colossus who, if the roof of the sky were to fall in, would hold it up with his two hands. It was the pepper, God spare you, and the torment in my heart. I yelled at him not knowing where I got my voice from. I said to him, "O Wad Maymouna", – and I showed my contempt for him by using his mother's name – "show yourself a man and strike with the whip. I swear that today they'll be carrying either you or me off to the graveyard."

'There was a hushed silence. He struck me the eighth, the ninth, the tenth stroke. He struck me with real hatred, as the strong man strikes when he knows he is weak, as the weak man strikes when he knows he is weak. When he'd reached thirty, your grandfather and Bandarshah, God bless them, got up and took the whip from his hand. "That's enough," they said. "You've had your due. It's Hamad's turn." Ah, my friend, I felt as though I were the Turkish generalissimo. I began to show off and strut about. I said to them, "Let him strike. I swear by the Chapter Kaf Lam Mim[18] – look what an absurb oath I swore by – they'll have to carry Wad

Maymouna off on a bier tonight." Your grandfather and Bandar-shah said, "Never − thirty strokes are enough." I took hold of the whip and found it was full of blood. God is great. I swished it around over the people present, as I took a couple of turns round the circle, prancing and strutting about.

'Wad Miftah al-Khazna and Wad Rahmatallah were quailing, looking down at the ground in fear. I flicked the whip above the heads of the two of them. Then I let out trilling cries of joy. Uwai, Uwai Uwaiyya! I looked at Mukhtar Wad Hasab ar-Rasoul and found that he was standing firm and solid, though the sweat was pouring from his forehead. I began circling round him and flicking him with the whip from time to time. I'd let out a scream and rush off, I would stand in front of him, then leap in the air. I waged a war of nerves against him till I was quite sure that my man was in a sorry state. Now, after having laughed at me, Wad Miftah al-Khazna and Wad Rahmatallah were on my side. Each time I laughed, they, − God punish them − laughed too − always with the winner. I raised the whip high and brought it down with a crack. God keep you safe, it was as if you'd torn a piece of cloth. Mukhtar didn't budge, but his eyes gave a blink. I brought down the next stroke and heard him grunt. I felt on top of the world. I gave him the third and he moved back slightly. At the fourth stroke he grew shaky. At the fifth he fell down in a faint. The people were as quiet as could be, not a sound, spellbound. I, the feeble and puny Hamad Wad Haleema defeating Mukhtar Wad Hasan ar-Rasoul, the doughty warrior, the dauntless hero!

'I tell you, I felt as though I were master of the universe, controller of the day and the night. We were just children, the eldest being no more than eight years old. I began striking out at random, now to the right, now to the left. I would strike this way and that, and the biggest beating I gave was to Wad Rahmatallah and Wad Miftah al-Khazna. I was possessed − I stood in the middle of the circle and put my foot on Mukhtar, who was lying lifeless on the ground, like a lion standing over its kill. I began talking gibberish − of which your grandfather and Bandarshah later reminded me. They said, "All right, that's enough." Your grand-father said to me, "All right, we know you're a man." Bandarshah replied to him, "If Wad Haleema thinks he's a man, there's a better one than him." All of a sudden, I felt a blow to the stomach from Bandarshah, after which I don't know what happened. When I woke up I found myself in Bandarshah's house on a low bed with

Mukhtar lying alongside me. What pain I was in, God spare you! I was screaming "Ay, ay" and Mukhtar was screaming "Ay, ay." '

CHAPTER FIVE

'**M**EHEIMEED.'
        Meheimeed turned towards the voice and called
out: 'Yes.'

Wad Rawwasi was surprised and said to him, 'Who are you answering?'

Immediately Meheimeed realized he had been immersed in a dream and had answered a call that no one had made.

Mahjoub got up and departed, while Abdul Hafeez left them and went on his way to the mosque.

'Poor Mahjoub,' said Wad Rawwasi. 'He's been defeated.'

The question had been on the tip of Meheimeed's tongue from the first night, but he didn't want to ask and had been hoping the answer would come of itself. He, Meheimeed, was also defeated, defeated by the days and defeated by the government. Sooner or later they would start asking him questions – most likely it will be Wad Rawwasi who will ask him 'What's made you retire when you haven't reached retirement age?' And Meheimeed will say to him 'They pensioned me off because I wouldn't perform the dawn prayers in the mosque.' Wad Rawwasi will say, 'Is that right or are you joking?' Meheimeed will say, 'In Khartoum now we've got a religious government: the Prime Minister daily performs the dawn prayers in person at the mosque, and if you don't pray, of if you pray on your own at home, they'll accuse you of a lack of fervour for the government. It's generous of them to put me on pension.'

'How extraordinary!' Wad Rawwasi will say in amazement.

'After a year or two or five,' Meheimeed will say to him, we'll be having a different government. Perhaps it will be non-religious. It might be atheistic. Then, whether you pray in your home or at the mosque, they'll pension you off.' Wad Rawwasi will say with great astonishment, 'On what grounds?' Meheimeed will say, 'On the grounds of having been in cahoots with the previous government.'

They won't believe their ears and they'll say with one voice, 'How extraordinary!'

Sa'eed had come out and seated himself on the bench alongside Taher Wad Rawwasi, while Meheimeed was stretched out on the sand, conscious of its coldness against his cheek and leg. Suddenly Sa'eed said, 'God's curse be on Bakri's boys! God willing, nothing will go right for them.'

Meheimeed was unable to contain himself any longer.

'What have Bakri's boys done?' he said.

Sa'eed Asha 'l-Baytat, in his call to prayer reached "Come to salvation", and he went on reiterating the phrase, making heavy weather of it like a lorry that had stuck in the sand, making up long vowels that were non-existent and disregarding those that were there.

Wad Rawwasi gave a laugh and said, 'Tonight the going is rougher than usual for Asha 'l-Baytat.'

Abdul Hafeez rose to his feet with a determination that astonished Meheimeed: it was as if, though wanting to remain seated, he had resolved to get up. Ever since Meheimeed had returned to Wad Hamid, Abdul Hafeez had been coming every night and saying nothing. He would come like someone apologizing, like someone wishing to divulge a secret.

The chasm of silence broadened out till it had filled with all those thoughts. Pursuing his enquiry, which had been all but lost, Sa'eed said, 'Bakri's son Tureifi is trying to make himself into a Bandarshah.'

In his imagination Meheimeed soared up with that awesome name, as it grew bigger and bigger like a giant genie amidst that darkness. And like a gigantic date palm that has no beginning or end round which parasitic creepers have twined, the winds of Amsheer[19] twined round that name, from bottom to top, from darkness to darkness. A name encircled by a feeling of gloom that was not born of this day. Where and when had he heard it before? Meheimeed remembered a certain person, rather a certain being, astride yesterday and tomorrow, holding a long whip on which were traces of blood, like Solomon[20] when he proceeded to chop off legs and heads. Was that it?

At supper Wad Rawwasi and Sa'eed took it in turns to relate the story to Meheimeed. Sa'eed was angry when he began and angry when he'd finished. Wad Rawwasi narrated it in the tone of someone who was no longer surprised at anything. They said that the story began with a dispute over land, for the mother of Bakri's boys was Mahjoub's sister. Mahjoub had thought the land to be his, but Bakri's boys suddenly stood up to him, and he was an old man, weakened by age, while they were young men at the peak of youth's callousness. They went on disputing with him for a whole year, taking him from court to court. They lost the land, but they smashed Mahjoub's power. They began to say openly the things that people had been saying in secret or not saying at all. It was as though the village was ripe for change. The whispers increased and the clamour grew louder and louder. Tureifi, Bakri's son would obstruct Mahjoub at meetings and would say within earshot of him 'This gang – Mahjoub and his group – when will they let go the reins of affairs in Wad Hamid? This group's finished. Enough that they've robbed the village for more than thirty years.' Such talk would anger Mahjoub, yet every action he took against them only served to lessen his prestige.

Wad Rawwasi asked sadly, 'What can an old and respected man do when a young ragamuffin picks a quarrel with him? If he hits him, people say, "This man's not to be taken seriously, he hits small boys," and if he lets him be, people say, "This worthless man isn't strong enough to curb a young ragamuffin." '

Sa'eed said that Mahjoub was a leader in Wad Hamid because of his abilities and because the village accepted him. That word 'acceptance' had great importance with Mahjoub and his group: they would say that So-and-so was 'acceptable' and that So-and-so had 'acceptability', which was in their view the highest praise. They then realized, as it were, all of a sudden, that the word no longer had any meaning and that that mysterious thing that makes a son submit to his father, a woman to her husband, the ruled to the ruler, and the young to the old, had vanished. It was as though the villagers had suddenly woken up from some old dream, or as though they had surrendered to a new one. People began looking at things with new eyes and with a variety of emotions which did not include acceptance.

Wad Rawwasi and Sa'eed said that the talk of Bakri's sons began to affect people's hearts. An opposition party was formed that started to grow stronger and more forceful, and they went about collecting signatures for holding a general meeting of the Co-operative, something that had not happened since its formation.

Their aim was to remove Mahjoub and his group from the Co-operative's committee and all the committees over which they had had control for thirty years. Mahjoub, after more than a quarter of a century of absolute power, found himself face to face with the people of Wad Hamid demanding an account from him.

The matter ended with the Co-operative being convened under the chairmanship of the Co-operative's chief inspector, who had come specially from Merowe for that memorable day. Wad Rawwasi said that Tureifi, Bakri's son, was the first to speak; he read out a long statement in which he included all the accusations that could possibly occur to anyone. He accused Mahjoub of corruption, bribery, theft, nepotism, incompetence, dereliction of duty, and so on. The speakers followed one another, all of them on the opposition side; among them were Seif ad-Din and Sa'eed the Owl (or Asha 'l-Baytat), who later held a banquet for the new committee. 'Naturally, seeing he became the treasurer. Can you believe it, Meheimeed, that Mahjoub's own sons voted against him? And that the girls made a demonstration in Wad Hamid calling for the downfall of Mahjoub and the gang of thieves?'

Sa'eed took up the thread of the story from Wad Rawwasi: 'Mahjoub sat listening to the accusations as though he were a wooden statue. Of our group only Taher and I were present. Abdul Hafeez, from the day he discovered the road to the mosque, gave up everything and washed his hands of it all. He said it was all futile. Ahmed, drunk as usual, didn't attend the meeting. Wad Rayyis, as you know, had died of a broken heart. Bakri's boys' mother, the sister of Mahjoub, came and stood amongst the men and cursed her sons roundly. The only word uttered by Mahjoub from the beginning of the meeting was when he chided his sister, saying, "Woman, go home." Something strange had occurred of which we didn't know the beginning or the end. Our children were against us. We had opened schools with sweat and effort and with running about here and there, and the outcome was that we had children who'd mix words with us. It seems that the village had got into a muddle right under our feet as we were sleeping the sleep of the just. Wad Rawwasi and I stood up and cursed the people one by one, by name, and reminded them of Mahjoub's favours towards them in the days when Mahjoub was the only one who was wide awake when the rest of the people were asleep. However, matters came to an end when they asked for a show of hands. The majority were against us. Under the big sayyal tree, in the middle of the village and in the middle of the day, Mahjoub was defeated. Mahjoub the tiger was defeated by hyenas – children, ragamuffins and impertinent, delinquent girls. They elected Tureifi the son of Bakri as president, Hasan the son of Bakri as vice-president and Hamza the son of Bakri as secretary, with Asha 'l-Baytat as treasurer, and with Seif ad-Din as works' controller – a new post for the purpose, they said, of improving work on the project. The girls in the demonstration, gave trilling cries of joy and Tureifi shouted, "Long live the people." Where are the people? Men like Asha 'l-Baytat, Wad Rahmatallah, Miftah al-Khazna, and so on? Are those the people?'

Wad Rawwasi wound up the story: 'Mahjoub got up from the meeting a finished man. He didn't utter a word. He didn't defend himself. He sat in silence and rose in silence. From that day on he walks the face of the earth as though dead. An era ended and a new era began in Wad Hamid. Till today we don't know how it all came about.'

Dragging his feet towards his house late at night, Meheimeed thought he knew the significance of that story, for he had seen it happen before in some remote, faraway time, and maybe he had been a part of it. In that story too, war was raging between what was and what would be. The Wad Hamid which he had carried about in his imagination all these years and which he had now returned to search for, like a soldier from a defeated army, no longer had any existence. His legs were feeling the weight of the fifty or sixty years, though his imagination was that of a child of less than ten. The jet-black night, the sayyal bushes crouching like women at a wake, the gleam of imagined lights in that pitch blackness, and the feeble sound of life in all that nothingness – and suddenly that call amidst the darkness: 'Meheimeed.'

A call close by, as close to him as his own jugular vein.[21]

'Yes,' said Meheimeed.

A clear, familiar voice, saying to him 'Come Meheimeed.'

He welcomed it and said yes, and it did not occur to him that it was an impossibility for the call was of the darkness or of the lightning that gleamed in the depth of the darkness, and he had no choice but to obey it and follow in its tracks.

CHAPTER SIX

I WALKED behind the voice in the depths of the darkness, not knowing whether I was walking backwards or forwards. My feet were plunging into the sand; then I had the sensation of travelling through air, swimming without effort, while the years slipped from my shoulders in the same way as one takes off one's clothes. There rose up in front of me a citadel with high towers, light blazing from its windows; it rose up like an island swimming in an ocean. I reached the door, the voice urging me on, and there found guards girded with daggers, who opened the door as though expecting my coming. I walked behind the voice down a long corridor of doors, a guard at each door, until we ended up in a vast hall lighted by thousands of lanterns, lamps and candles. In the centre of the hall facing the door was a raised dais on which was a throne with a chair to its right and another to its left, while on both sides people stood with bowed heads. The place was silent, not with an absence of noise but as though speech had yet to be created.

I followed the voice till I found myself standing before the person seated on the throne: a face of smooth blackness like velvet, and blue eyes that shone with cosmic cunning. It seemed to me that I had seen that face before in some age or other. 'We welcome our son Meheimeed,' said the voice, the very voice that had previously called to me and had guided me there, the voice, that of my grandfather – there was no doubt about it – the face of Bandarshah. How strange! A swift fleeting moment of realization passed through me during which I knew everything, as though in that moment I had understood the secret of life and the universe. But, just as it came, it was lost to me and I was no longer able to remember anything. I had no memory except of the magical name, Bandarshah. I looked, and there, to the right of the seated figure, was another version of it, as though it were he – and I understood.

I stood in bewilderment for a moment looking at the two images forming and dissolving. They would look alike as though they were a single original but no sooner were you sure of this than you were plunged into a sea of doubt. Is this a funeral or a wedding? Are we in the Hind or the Sind? In Omdurman or Isphahan?

Bandarshah indicated the empty chair to his left, so I seated myself. Then he clapped his hands and the soldiers brought eleven men, dragging their chains, who stood submissively in front of him, their eyes raised to him pleadingly. 'Father, pardon us and have mercy upon us,' they said in one voice.

The figure seated on the throne smiled and looked to his right, at his grandson Meryoud. The latter rose and went down from the dais, and he was brought long, thick whips made of the roots of the sant tree. The soldiers stripped the eleven men of their clothes and began dragging them along, one after the other, to Meryoud, who flogged each one of them while the figure on the throne listened and looked, smiled in satisfaction and gestured with his hand when he wished the flogging to be stopped or continued. Blood flowed in rivers from the backs of these eleven men as they suffered in silence, without so much as a cry or even a moan. The universe was silent: deaf, dumb and blind but for the whipcracks on the backs of Bandarshah's sons, within sight and earshot of their father, and performed by the grandson on behalf of the grandfather.

They were flogged until they drowned in their own blood. Bandarshah clapped his hands and the soldiers came and bore away the lifeless bodies. Then he clapped and the servants came with jugs of wine from which they filled a cup for Bandarshah, and one for Meryoud, and they presented me with one.

Bandarshah clapped a third time and naked maidens with jutting breasts entered the hall, their thighs and buttocks quivering, girls white and black and yellow and brown, from the Caucasus and Ahwaz, from the Caspian coast and the Ivory coast, their faces empty like masks, devoid of sensuality and feeling. They danced and sang and beat upon drums, tambourines and cymbals. Then Bandarshah yawned and in an instant the hall emptied and the three of us were alone, seated on that dais.

The silence lasted a long time as I looked at the splashes of blood and there rang in my ears the joyless echoes of drums and cymbals. I wanted Bandarshah to explain to me the significance of what had happened, but he said nothing and I finally realized that the voice had called me solely that I might be a witness.

CHAPTER SEVEN

SA'EED the Owl's voice as Meheimeed heard it at that hour, when in a state between sleep and wakefulness, was like a magnet which had attracted particles of unfulfilled dreams, so that it had taken on depths and dimensions it did not possess. It was not as he had heard it the first time, that weak, feeble voice. He leapt from his bed, made his ablutions, and left the house. The gusty winds of Amsheer blew in his face, almost bringing him to a standstill. He didn't know why he did this, for he hadn't performed the dawn prayer communally for thirty years or more.

He left his house and walked, his shoes plunging into the cold sand, the biting wind nipping him round the legs. He walked towards the mosque as his grandfather used to as though the call to prayer that dawn was meant for him alone, as though there were some debt he had to discharge, as though at last he was acting out a part that had been prepared for him and which he had shunned all these years.

On reaching the mosque, he found it crammed with people. At first sight he was astonished and asked Abdul Hafeez whether the crowd was because of some major happening that had occurred in the village.

'God guides aright him whom He will,' said Abdul Hafeez.

There was no doubt that Abdul Hafeez was happy because the piety trade was prospering that morning: there was Seif ad-Din, who oscillated between being on the right path and going astray; there, too, was Mukhtar Wad Hasab ar-Rasoul, who prayed only over the dead and who had risen from his bed and come to the mosque that dawn – under the influence of what power? And Hamad Wad Haleema, who used to say he'd divorced the road to the mosque in fury at the Imam – what had brought him now? And Abdul Maula Miftah al-Khazna, who used to say when asked about his having given up praying, 'Prayer's there for the asking and the road to the mosque is well known, and I'll go to the mosque when God lifts up my foot,' and Suleiman Akl an-Nabag would say to him, 'You're talking about the mosque as though it's across the sea in Mecca, not a few steps from your house.'

Both of them came that dawn, also Kashif Wad Rahmatallah, even at that early hour smart and well turned out, as though invited to a banquet. And Tureifi, the son of Bakri, the new leader, who came maybe to consecrate his victory over Mahjoub. Mahjoub, too, who had never in his whole life entered the mosque – had he come perhaps to seek divine help to overcome his defeat? And in the left-hand corner, under the window, there sat a man whose presence had its effect. Unable to make him out, Meheimeed asked Abdul Hafeez about him but he said he didn't know him.

As he looked closely at the man sitting under the window, Meheimeed was aware of that old sensation he had had, a mixture of fear, expectancy and composure. Suddenly, there flooded into his imagination complete and distinct images from the day he was circumcized. He had been six; he remembered the noise and the faces of the men and women going in and coming out of the houses, the animals that were slaughtered, and the trilling cries of the women; he remembered his grandfather holding him, and the knife, and that it was all done in an instant, before he had prepared himself for it, and the feeling of resentment, as though someone had struck him unexpectedly, and the excruciating pain that followed. There had been a preternatural feeling, as though a prophet had been born that dawn, or some miracle had taken place, or some cosmic catastrophe had occurred. Abdul Hafeez was sitting beside him. He spoke to him, but he didn't respond. Meheimeed turned and found that Abdul Hafeez was kneeling in prayer, and that he remained so for a long time. Then he heard him sobbing with suppressed crying. When he straightened up to the sitting position, he saw in the dim light that his face was moist with tears.

The Imam recited the Chapter of the Forenoon in a resounding voice that drew its strength from the sorrows of the men who had gathered that dawn, unexpectedly and without clear reason. Abdul Hafeez was at first weeping on his own, then he was joined by Seif ad-Din, then by Sa'eed Asha 'l-Baytat, then by Mahjoub, while, under the pressure of all that, Meheimeed wavered between doubt and certainty. In kneeling, he felt that he was almost there, but when he raised his head his heart was wholly empty. The crying then swelled and the wave carried the recited verses, verse after verse, fluttering on the surface like banners.

Meheimeed felt he was drowning and saw above the horizon the person who had been sitting under the window now sitting in the middle of the hall, as he had that night: black of colour, blue-eyed, holding the threads of chaos like a bright, destructive ray. There were inhabited homes, houses like fortresses, fields ripe with fruits, luxuriant trees and singing birds. Rivers flowed with milk and honey, and girls with jutting breasts, of all kinds and hues, danced and sang. The winds howled, bearing with them sparks and fire, and there were mourning women, and men fettered with chains, and the falling of whips upon living flesh. Bandarshah was sitting in the centre of the hall, listening and watching, while voices called out, 'Father, pardon us and have mercy upon us.' They were eleven brothers, slaves to what had passed and to what would not come about in a clearly defined form. One day they rebelled and destroyed the two of them together. Houses were made desolate, tracks were obliterated, and the soldiers came and led them off to prison.

Meheimeed awoke to Abdul Hafeez's voice saying to him, 'Ask forgiveness of God.' He found himself kneeling with a sensation of pain in his forehead and his face wet with tears. He rose to the sitting position and said 'Peace be upon you',[22] in a frightened tone, and found that the people had finished their prayers and he alone had remained kneeling. They were all looking at him in astonishment. At once he turned towards the window where the stranger had been and found that he wasn't there. He ran towards where he had been but there was no one there. He screamed at the top of his voice, 'Have you seen the man who was here?' Some said yes, some no, but no one had seen him when he had gone out.

CHAPTER EIGHT

THAT night it seemed as if time had taken a great turn backwards. It was a warm night and the moon was full. In his heart, Meheimeed felt an energy like that of days of old. Mahjoub was present and Abdul Hafeez was present, also Ahmed and Taher and the two Sa'eeds, the Owl and the Jurist. Sa'eed the Owl was the pivot. Meheimeed knew that before the meeting broke up that night they would ask him and that he would recount to them the story without bitterness, as though it had happened to someone else.

'Friends, I want to resign from the committee,' said Sa'eed the Owl with a laugh. 'This business of being treasurer is nothing but a headache.'

The strange thing was that Mahjoub also laughed and said to Sa'eed, 'You and Seif ad-Din and Bakri's boys think it's all child's play – you can take your fill of it yourselves now.'

'The day of the meeting of the Co-operative,' said Taher to Sa'eed, 'didn't you, you good-for-nothing Asha 'l-Baytat, lend your voice to those who spoke out against Mahjoub, saying he was this and that? That we were a gang of thieves who'd plundered the village? Now you too can have a go.'

'How eloquent Asha 'l-Baytat was!' said the other Sa'eed – and his laugh was almost back to what it used to be – 'Since God created me, I've not heard its like! That day, though I was so furious I was nearly bursting, when Asha 'l-Baytat got up to speak, God keep you safe, if it hadn't been for the solemnity of the occasion, I'd have burst out laughing. Do you remember, you Asha of dust and ashes, what you said that day?'

Sa'eed laughed at this and Mahjoub said, 'God keep you safe, I had my answer to all the accusations ready. I wanted to make a laughing-stock of Bakri's son in front of all the people and not leave him a leg to stand on. When I heard what Asha 'l-Baytat had to say, I told myself "Hold your tongue – the thing's become ridiculous, a game for kids." May God keep you safe, after that, even if they'd given me a million pounds, I wouldn't have accepted the job.'

'Mahjoub,' said Sa'eed, 'you're talking rubbish. By the testimony of faith, the whole thing's burning into the depths of your heart. Now, if this very day they were to call you to the committee, you'd run so fast there'd be no catching you. Brothers, why are you so greedy? Fine, you've had your share, so allow us to try out our luck for two or three years.'

'Weren't you saying a short time ago that you were resigning?' said Ahmed.

'Meheimeed,' said Taher, 'have you seen that hypocritical good-for-nothing Asha? God keep you safe, there were times when he didn't have the wherewithal to buy his children's supper. Ask him, go on, ask him, who besides Mahjoub and his gang of thieves gave him so much as a glance?'

'The problems of his divorce and marriages alone,' said Abdul Hafeez, 'needed a committee to sort them out.'

Sa'eed Asha 'l-Baytat laughed and said, 'I didn't do any wrong where you were concerned. In front of all the people I acknowledged the good deeds you'd all done. It's a matter of free choice. People said, "Out with Mahjoub and his lot; in with Tureifi and Asha 'l-Baytat." What more is there to it?'

'Well, let us see if Bakri's boys will be of any use to you,' said Mahjoub.

Directing his words at Mahjoub, Asha 'l-Baytat said laughing. 'Have a fear of God, Mahjoub. Do you want to make yourself into a Bandarshah in the place?'

Meheimeed told himself that Sa'eed didn't know what he was saying, but the name had started to float on the surface and would continue to recur in this way without warning until things became real, if there was any reality; otherwise it would go as it came, from darkness into darkness.

'Don't worry about all that,' said Taher. 'Tell us what you said at the meeting.'

Said Sa'eed Asha 'l-Baytat, the pivot on that moonlit night, 'Meheimeed, those friends of yours have contempt for people and no knowledge of the truth. They say: "Sa'eed the Owl". Fattouma sang and said: "Asha 'l-Baytat, the islands' crocodile." By the sentence of faith, the call to prayer I made was made for God

37

Almighty's sake, and the work on the committee is nothing but pain and grief. By the sentence of the faith at the present time I don't care about any committee or project, or even about the governor of the province.'

Remembering his conversation previously with Sa'eed, Meheimeed said to him, 'Maybe you found yourself some buried treasure?'

'They say Sa'eed found himself some treasure,' said Ahmed, 'or how is it you put on all those fine airs, you miserable creature?'

'May God be pleased with you, O Haneen our Sheikh,' said Sa'eed.

'May God keep you safe,' said Mahjoub, 'there wasn't any treasure or any trove. It's the Headmaster's money he's squandering.'

Sa'eed laughed and didn't reply.

'They say Sa'eed wants to divorce the Headmaster's daughter,' said Ahmed.

'I shan't divorce the Headmaster's daughter,' said Sa'eed, 'but I wouldn't mind marrying again if the opportunity came my way.'

'Who would ever accept you, you good-for-nothing?' said Abdul Hafeez. 'Do you think yourself still young?'

'He should find himself one of those educated girls who've sprung up,' said Mahjoub. 'One who speaks English – English is all the rage now.'

Taher said: 'One of those girls who called out at that demonstration, "Long live the people." And who are the people if not the likes of good-for-nothing Asha 'l-Baytat?'

Meheimeed was exceedingly surprised when Sa'eed Asha 'l-Baytat said with conviction, 'By the sentence of the faith, the place is doing fine, it's getting along all right. You're the sort of people who say, if you're not in charge, the place has gone to the dogs. Yes, long live the people. The people are us. Good luck to the girls who demonstrate: modest, polite and well-educated. Our daughters and the daughters of our sons. And if I found one of them who'd marry me, by the sentence of the faith, I'd do it tomorrow.'

Meheimeed's astonishment was greater still when no one laughed at Sa'eed's words or protested at them. It was as though the moon were somehow smiling, and the light were a spring that would never dry up, and the sounds of life in Wad Hamid were harmonious and cohesive, giving you the sensation that death was no more than another of life's meanings. Everything is and will continue to be. No war will break out, no blood will be spilt. Women will give birth without pain, the dead will be buried without weeping, and change will come about in the same way as the seasons change in a temperate clime, season in front of season, season behind season, all swimming in an orbit, the night not outstripping the day. It was a wonderful silence, all the more wonderful because it had come about unexpectedly.

'God is alive,' said Abdul Hafeez.

Meheimeed thought that one of these three might play a heroic role: Sa'eed because he was devoid of ambition, his shop was the same, neither more nor less: eating the same things, dressing in the same way and grumbling as he had always done for more than forty years; quick to anger and quick to laughter as he always was. And Taher Wad Rawwasi because he laughed both at himself and at others, and his loyalty was not to himself but to Mahjoub. As for the other Sa'eed, he was a man of his time and his star was in the ascendant. Whatever happened they had roles that they had not as yet played out. Mahjoub had played out his role and was finished; his was the real tragedy because he didn't want to leave the stage.

Taher Rawwasi gave a deep sigh and said, 'Time comes and Time goes.'

Sa'eed the Jurist laughed and said, 'I'll tell you what Asha 'l-Baytat said at the Co-operative meeting – they should print his speech in books and study it at school. Listen Meheimeed – pay attention well. Ahmed and Abdul Hafeez weren't present. The people were jam-packed under the sayyal tree. The heat was stifling and we were gathered for a fight to the death. Then our friend – you know who – stands up to make a speech. The night before he had dined with us. He'd sworn that he'd vote with us. The moment he got up I said to Wad Rawwasi, "Never mind, it's all one – he may be a stupid idiot but even so he's with us." Not a "Peace be upon you", or "In the name of God", or "Thanks be to God" – he started right off with, "Good people, Mahjoub and the likes of Taher and Sa'eed are my friends and my folk. Mahjoub's a great person, saving your presences. By the sentence of faith, he's a man worth the weight of a thousand men, a man of valour and a man of honour. But the truth must be told, the group plundered the village; they picked away at the flesh and left nothing but the bone. Ruination its been. From the time God created us the group's been ravaging and plundering. Everything was permissible to them. What they plundered no one wants to take back from them. May God keep you safe, yet they were people you could rely on in good times and bad. But, the devil take them, they ravaged and pillaged the village. They were rapacious men and their bellies were never satisfied. Now, as the leader, Tureifi the son of Bakri, has said: Let these people go off to their homes without fuss. If on the other hand they've got something to say, then the people are ready and waiting for them. Up the people. Long live the people. Long live Tureifi. Down with Mahjoub – and especially down with the son of Ismail, may God wipe out all mercy to him and nothing go right for him. That fellow's stupidly generous and all his money goes on arak. Mahjoub's a grand person, saving your presences, a man who served the village but also ravaged and plundered it. He sold me clover at fifty piastres the haud.[23] I said to him: "I'll be partners with you in the cow." He said: "I don't want any partnership." Fellows, praise the Prophet: what's lawful is plain and what's unlawful is plain.[24] Put an end to this matter and let's all go home.'

The person who laughed the most was Asha l'Baytat himself. Almost choking with laughter, he said, 'Didn't I give every man his due? Correct or not?' And suddenly, in the midst of his gaiety, he said, 'Friends, I want to tell you a secret I haven't told a soul.' With difficulty he gained their attention and said, 'It was last winter in Amsheer. It was cold and windy, between night and dawn. Don't ever think it was a dream. I saw it with my own eyes, just as I'm seeing you now. Brothers, by the life of your brotherhood, I was awake and the lamp was lit. I was covered with three blankets and the wind outside was screaming "wai wai wai". The windows were closed and the door was closed. In the name of God the Merciful, the Compassionate, I take refuge in God from the accursed devil. He stood above my bed and said to me sharply, "Rise". It was our Sheikh Haneen, may God be pleased with him. When I'd got rid of my fear, I looked carefully at him: it was him all right, wearing his cloak and with his shawl over his shoulders and his unmistakable ewer in his hand. He said to me, "Rise". I said to him, "Where to, Sheikh?" He said to me, "Walk to the castle." I said to him, "To the ruins?" He said to me, "They're not ruins. Walk to the castle and you'll find a palace." I said to him, "Whose palace?" He said to me, "Bandarshah's palace." I said to him, "And who would Bandarshah be?" He said to me, "One of the sultans of olden times. He lived long, long ago. He had endless properties and lands. He had fields in which horses would gallop without ever reaching the boundaries. So much dates, wheat and corn that they found difficulty harvesting them. He had one son and eleven slaves. Walk to the palace on the hill and you'll find an open door. Enter and walk on till you enter the diwan.[25] There you will find Bandarshah and his son awaiting you. They have something for you that has been kept in trust. Do not greet them. Do not talk to them. Do not turn to right or to left. Go in, take what they give you and go. Be very careful not to say a single word: you would enter the abode of destruction and he who looks for you would not find you. The thing kept in trust is wealth. It is your inheritance by right. Bandarshah thought of himself as inheriting the earth and all that was on it. The earth is your earth and the earth of the meek after you. Rise. Rise."

'My friends, I walked to the castle and there it was just as our Sheikh Haneen had described it to me. A palace — and what a palace! God be my witness, it was all lit up, you'd have said it was a statement — and the sound of singing and dancing and laughter. I walked, turning neither to left nor to right, feeling as though girls were grabbing at me from this side and from that. The diwan was no doubt full of women; I didn't turn and I didn't look, but there was an unmistakable perfume of mahaleb and sandalwood diffused throughout the place. I found the two of them sitting, God be my witness, as though they were a king and his vizier. The old man said to me, "Greetings and welcome. Welcome to our son Asha 'l-Baytat. Sit down, drink and enjoy yourself." I didn't answer him. I stretched out my hand, my thoughts in turmoil. The young boy spoke, saying, "Say something. Answer our greeting." God keep you safe, I almost spoke, but the good Lord saved me. I was utterly silent. The old man clapped his hands. A young girl like a houri came in. Her breasts had only just begun to grow and were the size of the berries of the laloub tree; stark naked she was, swaying about. Her buttocks were as smooth as lizard skin, her belly like the orchards of Shaygiyya. She grasped me by my thing and said, "Come to me, I'm ready for you." She lay down and opened her thighs and I saw what she had and what she could give. She said to me "Come, light of my eyes, and lie between my thighs. There you'll attain the heights of joy." Ah, brothers, what fires were raging in me! With my two eyes I saw the path to salvation and the path to perdition. Had it not been for God's providence I would have fallen into the direst of calamities, and I wouldn't have cared. Under my breath I sought refuge from the accursed devil and said, "O Helper!" and I stretched out my hands, deaf and dumb as our Sheikh Haneen had exhorted me. The young boy stood up and stamped his foot in annoyance and scolded the girl, who immediately took herself off. The old man laughed and said to him, "Don't be angry, Meryoud. He's an inheritor, coming for his due. Hand over to him what has been held in trust and let him depart unharmed." The boy handed over to me a purse, which I took and passed on as I had entered, without a farewell or uttering a single word. When I came to, I found myself at the mosque: cold and sweating and weeping as a she-camel does for her young from which she has been parted. Dawn was about to break. I didn't open the purse or look inside it. I placed it by the prayer-niche. Then I went up the minaret, crying I know not for what or over what. From sadness was it? Or from joy? I gave the call to prayer, brother, and the voice did not come out as my own. It was a voice full of sorrows. I gave the call over the housetops; I called to the water-wheels and the trees; I called to the sand-dunes and to the graves; to those present and to those absent; I called to those that are astray and to the defeated, to the broken, to the sober and to the drunk. I called to the Christians and the Moslems. I called "God is great. God is great", weeping and wailing and not knowing whether I was weeping and wailing for what I had gained or for what I had lost. Ah, friends, what a night that was! I heard with my own ears the winds of Amsheer echoing my call to prayer, as though I the miserable, puny Sa'eed was the Bandarshah of my time, saying to the people of this world and the next "Come to perdition. Come to success. Come to error. Come to salvation". Up in the minaret at dawn I had the feeling that the angels and the devils were saying with one voice, "Amen. Amen." I came down to find the mosque filled with people – Mahoud and Masood, Khair ad-Din and Seif ad-Din, Mahjoub and Alloub, Meheimeed and Abu 'l-Waleed, Wad Hasab ar-Rasoul, Wad Bakri, Wad Rahmatallah and Wad Miftah al-Khazna – people who'd never been inside the mosque before. It was as though the whole village had gathered together at dawn in the mosque. I knew, brothers, that they had all gathered together because they had heard the voice. The person calling had called them with my tongue. There was something out of the ordinary that dawn. Prayers were held and my tears fell in buckets. The Imam recited the Chapter of the Forenoon. I heard the weeping of Abdul Hafeez, and Seif ad-Din, and then Mahjoub and Meheimeed, while I wept and drew them along behind me, until all those praying were weeping warm tears that dawn. Why and for what? Ah! Ah! At the left-hand window was a stranger who had some connection with all that had taken place, disappearing and reappearing until the people said "Peace be upon you". He vanished without trace and poor Meheimeed was shouting at the top of his voice saying, "Where's the person who was here gone to?"

'In the house I lit the lamp before the light of morning appeared. Opening the purse, I found all sorts of things, as though they were the treasure troves of King Solomon, God's omnipotence be exalted! I turned them over in my hands without any sense of delight or joy, as though I were rummaging about in ashes. I threw it down somewhere in the house, I don't know where, and slept the sleep of the dead for the whole day. Waking from sleep, I wept copious tears, not knowing the why or the wherefore.'

There was in Sa'eed's voice as he recounted that story, something that filled those men with a feeling of anguish so that they gave themselves up to a deep, extensive silence, to be broken at length by Abdul Hafeez's voice saying, 'God is alive.'

Silence reigned again and Mahjoub, Sa'eed and Ahmed all sighed. Suddenly Wad Rawwasi gave a bellow of laughter and said, 'May God keep you safe, it's mere hallucination. You're making fools of us, Asha 'l-Baytat, with talk that's like the riddles of olden times. It seems that going up the minaret at dawn has affected your mind. Tomorrow you'll be coming along and telling us that you're God's prophet the Khidr, or the Awaited Mahdi!'

Then they all laughed, with the exception of Meheimeed. Said Ahmed Ismail, nicknamed Abu 'l-Banat, 'That's drunken talk. Asha 'l-Baytat must have been drunk. I swear that after drinking a bottle of arak one's like what's-his-name Shahbandar or Bandarshah.'

Sa'eed did not protest and said no more than 'Ah!' and then again 'Ah, ah, ah!'

Meheimeed was the only one who believed, under the spell of the all-encompassing light that night, that Asha 'l-Baytat had indeed seen and heard all that he had described. And if it was a dream, then it would rise like a flood till it drowned the whole village.

'Dawn's nearly breaking,' said Abdul Hafeez. 'Off you go, Asha 'l-Baytat – get up the minaret and give the call to prayer.'

Sa'eed, happy and in a good mood, floated up from his silence, and it was in this state that he said to them, 'What do you say to all of us getting up and attending the dawn prayers, seeing that today's Friday? After prayers you're all invited to have breakfast with me in the diwan of His Honour the Headmaster. I've got a fat lamb we can slaughter and we can make a good meal of it.'

The first one to accept the invitation was Ahmed.

'If there's going to be mutton after prayers,' he said, 'I've got no objection.'

Taher Wad Rawwasi refused, so did Sa'eed the Jurist and Meheimeed. Mahjoub, though, suddenly said, 'By God, what Asha 'l-Baytat says makes good sense – a prayer and a party all in one. Let's go, men.'

His voice was as in the days when he had been the captain of the ship, he giving the orders and they carrying them out. At that instant they were reunified as had not happened for a long time. That was why, as they moved off into the rising dawn, between light and darkness, Taher Rawwasi said, 'God's mercy be upon you, Wad Rayyes.'[1]

They got up and walked behind Sa'eed Asha 'l-Baytat, making their way to prayers like people going to a feast.

CHAPTER NINE

T HE evening gathering broke up with the blood that was spilt having splashed over everyone. Love died or almost did. The sun was rising and setting, the moon going up and down, the wind blowing, the river running, the village going to sleep and waking up. Everything had lost its taste and meaning. A month after the incident occurred I found the three of them in my grandfather's house, stretched out on those beds, lifeless, exchanging not a word: no conversation, no greeting. I stayed on a long time, waiting, turning things over in my mind and trying to understand the significance of what had happened. I recalled that forenoon when Meryoud had come buying and selling, having been deputed to do so by Bandarshah. How similar are miracles to disasters!

I deliberately flouted the rule of good behaviour which commanded me to keep silent, in an attempt to provoke them.

'It's Bandarshah who's responsible,' I suddenly shouted out. 'If it hadn't been for him, it wouldn't have happened.'

Each one of them answered my insolence with a slight nervous movement and kept silent. Many had been killed, so why should they trouble to mourn a particular one?

'It's said that the two of them put up an astounding struggle.'

'Who,' answered Wad Heleema grimly at once, 'heard or saw anything so as to be able to say?'

I wanted to draw them out of their silence by any means.

'I heard people talking,' I said.

But they maintained their silence.

'God curse them' said my grandfather.

Out of all the people of the village, Hamad Wad Haleema had been the nearest to the centre of the chaos on that forenoon and for sure his heart was seething in turmoil. If he were to speak now, his two friends would too. Directing my words at him, I said. 'You were the first, were you not, to come upon Bandarshah?'

Mukhtar Wad Hasab ar-Rasoul violently puffed air from his mouth, while Wad Haleema gave a groan.

'An accursed time,' said my grandfather.

No doubt the hour of doom seemed to them to be imminent. I thought sorrowfully that those three men would have preferred death to life at that moment. Their life-span had brought them to a time when they saw the world submerged in a flood of sin. After the Bandarshah incident many of their generation had died suddenly, and whenever my grandfather heard of the death of one of his contemporaries he would give a sorrowful sigh. Certainly some extraordinary things had occurred after that incident. Al-Kashif Wad Rahmatallah, despite being well advanced in years, suddenly decided to leave the village; the Imam refused to take the people in prayer and said they were all doomed and that neither prayer nor admonition would avail them, after which he took himself off to Mecca to die there. Bakri's wife, after fifty years of marriage, left her husband's house with head bared, swearing not to return. Those who weren't rebellious rebelled, and those who weren't quarrelsome quarrelled, and people said that devils had begun to walk in the squares and streets, openly in broad daylight.

'It's said,' I said to them, 'that they tied the two of them up with ropes, each one of them to a chair in the centre of the diwan.'

Wad Hasab ar-Rasoul gave a sigh and so did Wad Haleema.

'God's curse be on the lot of them,' said my grandfather.

'It's said that they beat them with whips made out of sant roots,' I said to them.

My grandfather suddenly sat bolt upright and said, 'Meaning to say it wasn't by stragulation or stabbing?'

'It's said,' I said to them, 'that he fought back like a lion and almost got the better of his eleven sons.'

In a hurt, subdued voice Mukhtar Wad Hasab ar-Rasoul said, 'He was ever a giant – a man of another clay.'

Yes, he was a texture all of his own, and his grandson had been fashioned in his form so as to be an extension of him, and he had vested him with absolute authority over his eleven sons, so that the two of them ruled with force and cunning, without love. All that became clear later. The two of them had a capacity that was superhuman.

'It's said,' I said to them, 'that Meryoud used to assign to each one of them the work he was to do and would fix his wage, not the slightest detail escaped his attention. Every night a court would be held in the large diwan. The two of them – Bandarshah, with Meryoud on his right – would sit on two high chairs placed on a dais in the centre of the diwan. They would give judgement together and the punishment would be by flogging, which Meryoud would administer, while Bandarshah sat cross-legged in his chair, listening and watching. Did you know that?'

No one replied to my question and I wondered how a man could have a black skin and blue eyes, and how one man could bring forth eleven sons, boy after boy, then choose his only grandson, to the exclusion of all of his sons to be his shadow on earth. Either that did not actually take place or it took place in some long past time, in the days when catastrophes and miracles used to occur.

'It's said,' I said to them, 'that the grandfather and the grandson used to drink wine together and that slave-girls would sing for them and dance naked at night in the large diwan in the midst of the houses. Did you know that?'

No one replied to my question, and I imagined to myself the closely packed houses, as though they were an impregnable fortress on a high hill, far from the rest of the quarter. It was a world on its own.

'It's said,' I said to them, 'that Meryoud used to interfere in their most intimate affairs and was charged to do so by Bandarshah – they weren't even free to marry off their own daughters.'

'I bear witness that there is no god but God,' said my grandfather.

'And I bear witness that Mohammed is the Messenger of God,'[26] said Hamad Wad Haleema.

'It is said,' I said to them, 'that Meryoud would wake them up at dawn and lock the courtyard gate on them at sundown; in all things he and Bandarshah drove them around like sheep.'

They fidgeted restlessly and said nothing.

'It is said,' I said to them, 'that Bandarshah excluded all his sons from his inheritance, registering all his property in the name of Meryoud. He said that the lot of them weren't worth a nail-clipping from Meryoud.'

Suddenly Wad Hasab ar-Rasoul sat upright and exclaimed, 'You listen to the talk of riff-raff like Wad Jabr ad-Dar, Wad Miftah al-Khazna and Wad Rahmatallah. Just because he's dead and gone they say that Bandashah was this and that. Bandarshah was unique among men. He was a man of another metal. Bandarshah drinking wine? I swear by God that Bandarshah never drank wine in his whole life – nor did anything base.'

Suddenly the three of them got up and went out, leaning on each other, leaving me on my own in the room, as though in a cemetery. I was angry and I was sad and I was in a state of great perplexity.

CHAPTER TEN

S TRETCHED out on his back and looking up at the ceiling, Taher Wad Rawwasi said, 'You know, fellows, this world is going the wrong way round. You, Meheimeed, wanted to be a farmer and you've become an effendi,[27] while Mahjoub wanted to be an effendi and became a farmer.'

Mahjoub's health had improved in recent times and he no longer complained of asthma, so he had stopped performing the dawn prayer in the mosque. He laughed and said, 'God keep you safe, if I'd been able to I'd have gone ahead with this education business, and no one would have caught up with me. I'd have become a governor or a minister.'

'This business of being a minister is child's play,' said Taher. 'In these times anyone at all can become a minister. By God, if Tureifi Walad Bakri doesn't become a minister, then I'm not the son of my father.'

'Where would they get him a ministry from?' said Meheimeed. 'There's not a single vacant ministry left.'

'They're never at a loss,' said Taher. 'They'd make him Minister of Charitable Societies or Minister of Pharmacies or Minister of Locomotives – any one of the kind of nonsenses we hear of.'

'Tureifi Walad al-Bakri,' said Mahjoub, 'isn't even capable of handling the Co-operative. Do you want to make him a minister as well?'

'Do you think it's a matter of ability?' said Taher. 'It's all bluff and show. The great thing is to spout a lot and to do nothing. Just say a lot of "up withs" and "long lives". See which party is strong and join it. A bit of speechifying, a bit of party-holding, a few backhanders. Slowly, slowly, you find you've become a member of parliament. After that just sit back on your bottom.'

'And if after you've got into parliament,' Meheimeed said to him, 'they don't make you a minister, what then?'

'If they don't make me a minister,' said Wad Rawwasi, 'I swear, I'd make a coup against them.'

'And then?' said Mahjoub.

'And then what?' said Taher. 'Why, that's it. Sit back on your bottom. Anything you want, just ring the bell. Come in, So-and-so. Beat it, So-and-so. So-and-so, I've appointed you Commandant of Police. So-and-so, I've made you Inspector-General. So-and-so, you've fallen out of favour with me and I'm putting you in prison. So-and-so, don't let me see your face again. So-and-so, you're a great fellow. When I pass in the Chevrolet through the town, the people will cheer, "Long live Taher Wad Rawwasi! Up with Taher Wad Rawwasi!" I'd have become a governor-general.'

Mahjoub guffawed and said, 'The devil take you – are you saying that governing is ringing a bell and saying "Come in, So-and-so, and beat it, So-and-so?'

'For your information,' said Meheimeed, 'the car wouldn't be a Chevrolet. If you put a Chevrolet alongside it, it would be like a donkey beside a horse.'

'There's no power except through Him,' said Wad Rawwasi. 'Is there anything even bigger than a Chevrolet?'

'Oh yes,' said Meheimeed.

'How big?' said Taher.

'As big as this diwan,' said Meheimeed.

'There is no power or strength except through Him,' said Taher. 'God keep you safe, if it's like that, consider me as from tomorrow nominating myself for the Presidency.'

The three of them laughed as they lay stretched out on those very beds, in that very diwan, at siesta time.

'Ah, my friend, give thanks to God,' said Meheimeed. 'What's a governor and what's a minister? You're better off than all of them. You've not got a worry in the world – nobody wants anything from you and you want nothing from anybody.'

Mahjoub gave a deep sad sigh.

'By God, you're right,' said Taher. 'So long as one knows where one's supper's coming from, God keep you safe, what does being a chief of police or a supreme commander matter? The problem is you, Meheimeed. You've given your life to studying, you've been about, and you've come back to this God-forsaken Wad Hamid with empty hands. It's as if you became an effendi by mistake. For a long time your heart's been in this miserable business of farming.'

Meheimeed also gave a sigh as he lay stretched out on his grandfather's bed at siesta time. After thinking for a long time, he said, 'What you say is right. Mahjoub should have gone along that road. Mahjoub has ambition. He wants power. But I want truth – and what a difference there is between searching for power and searching for truth.'

Wad Rawwasi laughed scornfully and said, 'Meaning to say you've come to this God-forsaken Wad Hamid because its got the truth? By God, what a laugh!'

'It's not a matter of truth,' said Mahjoub. 'It's a matter of stupidity. Meheimeed and I were in the same class at the elementary school. Do you remember? I was the brightest in the class. Meheimeed was way back. My father, God rest his soul, said, "That's enough. No need for schools and all that nonsense." That year people were hard put to it to reap the wheat. He said, "Come along – work with us just like everybody else." Meheimeed's father, God bless him, said the same thing. His grandfather, though, had made up his mind and said not a bit of it, he should go along with school till he saw the end of the road. And what was the end? Meheimeed, having gone all over the place, has come back to farming as though, as the saying goes, "O Badr, it's as if we never came and never went." '

'He was an authoritarian who always got his way,' said Taher. 'Once he'd made up his mind, nothing would shift him, whatever the cost. God rest his soul.'

'After that everything went wrong.' said Meheimeed. 'One has to say no from the very beginning. I was happy in Wad Hamid. By day I'd cultivate the land and at night I'd serenade the girls. I'd snare birds and splutter around in the Nile like a hippo. One's heart was free and at peace. I became an effendi because my grandfather wanted me to. When I became an effendi I wanted to become a doctor. Instead I became a teacher. When I was teaching, I told them I'd like to work in Merowe, so they told me to work in Khartoum. In Khartoum, I told them I'd like to teach boys, but they told me to teach girls. In the girls' school I told them I'd like to teach history, so they told me to teach geography. In geography I told them I'd like to teach Africa, so they told me to teach Europe. And so on and so forth.'

Wad Rawwasi laughed heartily.

'People have no sense,' he said. 'God keep you safe, if I'd been you I'd have made a revolution against them.'

'I wish,' said Mahjoub, 'we could organize ourselves a revolution that would shift Tureifi from the chairmanship of the Co-operative.'

Suddenly the question came. Wad Rawwasi sat bolt upright, looked at Meheimeed and said to him, 'Meheimeed, you're quite certainly younger than me and Mahjoub. I don't think you've reached retirement age. How come they pensioned you off before your time?'

Meheimeed remembered the story about praying and laughed.

'Yes,' said Mahjoub, 'what happened?'

'When things came to a head,' said Meheimeed, 'I went off to the people in authority and said to them, "I've had enough. I don't want any more of it. I don't want to serve any more. Give me my entitlements and let me go back to the house of my father and grandfather, to plough and cultivate the land like the rest of God's people; to drink water from a pitcher and eat a crust of bread with okra grown on the river banks; to lie on my back at night in the courtyard of the diwan looking at the sky above, so wonderfully clear and with the moon gleaming like a silver dish." I told them, "I want to return to the past, to the days when people were people and Time was Time." I told them, "That's enough, take what's owing to you and give me my rights. This is the parting of the ways." '

'And what did they say to you, Meheimeed?' asked Wad Rawwasi. 'They say the homegrown rulers are a tough bunch, God spare you. In the days of the English he'd tell you off and say "Get out." Now the homegrown one gives you a kick up the backside.'

'There's no hitting and no kicking,' said Meheimeed, laughing. 'Everything's done nicely and properly. Formalities are followed according to laws and regulations and letters: "It is with regret that we inform, you" and "we are pleased to notify you." For a month I sat at home. They then arranged matters, as they say, amicably. It so happened that I had a year to go so they counted it in for me and then it was: Peace be upon you and upon you be peace.'

'And as you were leaving, you didn't give anyone two or three slaps just to work off your spleen?'

'Meheimeed's not a man for resorting to blows,' said Mahjoub.

'What's the point of violence?' said Meheimeed. 'The thing's all done sensibly.'

'And your sons and daughters, Meheimeed?'

'The boys have been taken by the government,' said Meheimeed with a touch of sadness, 'and the girls have been taken by effendis. Good luck to them. They've entered the world of cars, fridges, and posts and grades. If they want to come here, they're welcome; if they want to stay there, I'll regard them as being a gift from me to the age of freedom, civilization and democracy. As for me, Wad Rawwasi, I'm an effendi by mistake; I'm a farmer, as you said, who wandered around aimlessly and returned to the starting-point. I've returned so as to be buried here. I swear I won't give my body to any earth other than that of Wad Hamid.'

Wad Rawwasi laughed and said, 'Meheimeed, you're either a poet or you're in your dotage. Nevertheless you're very welcome. Wad Hamid is a God-forsaken place. In summer its heat is unbearable, and in the winter − God spare you − so is its cold. There are gnats at the time of the pollination of the dates and flies when the millet comes out. It has snakes and scorpions, malaria and dysentery. Its life is one of toil and trouble, its troubles as numerous as the hairs on your head. Ask us, we've had good experience of it. There are screams when you're born and screams when you die. Your Honour's life has been spent reclining in an office under a fan. Water comes from a tap, lighting is by electricity, and travel's first class. My! My! You haven't stood about making channels for water in the depths of winter. You haven't ridden donkeys till your arse swelled up. You haven't sat around watching the dates when they're ripening, praying to God He won't send down rain or a gale on them. You haven't guarded the wheat with your hand on your heart for fear of birds or the pest getting at it. And now, with the south wind changing direction for you, you've come looking for a lie-down in the diwan so that you can gaze up at the moon sparkling in the seventh heaven. A thousand welcomes to you and make yourself at home.'

'Well said, Wad Rawwasi,' said Mahjoub, laughing.

And Meheimeed laughed as he hadn't laughed for years, a thin, squeaky laugh.

'Wad Rawwasi,' he said, 'you're more of a poet than I am.'

CHAPTER ELEVEN

I RECKONED that Tureifi must have been thirty-six or thirty-seven, for he was around twelve in the year of the wedding of Zein. At that time Mahjoub was forty-five – I know that for a fact – while Ahmed, who today has become the father of many daughters and whose daughters are of marriageable age, was about twenty in that year. I scrutinized his face as he sat in front of me on the verandah of the diwan, cross-legged, holding a cup of coffee, in the forenoon. There was nothing remarkable about the face apart from the narrow, intelligent eyes and that ironic smile at the left-hand corner of the mouth that speaks of a contradiction between what he says and what he means. There was also something else: that thing that power bestows on those who have it, a mixture of daring and fear, of generosity and greed, of timidity and boldness, of truth and falsehood. It was as though you were confronted by an actor performing a part; you know that what is taking place before you is not real yet you cannot help but give yourself up to the illusion. Tureifi was fully aware of the nature of the role he was performing.

He ended his speech by saying: 'The world must go forwards not backwards. There is no doubt that you of all people realize that. Mahjoub has performed his role and that's that. We too will perform ours.'

I recollected that Tureifi was not only the son of Mahjoub's sister but was also the husband of his daughter.

He also said: 'Mahjoub and his gang imagined they had a divine right to authority. They forgot the village had changed. Many things have happened. Wad Hamid is no longer the Wad Hamid of thirty years ago. New generations have appeared, new demands. In the old days, when the steamer appeared people would gather under the doum[28] tree and look at it as though it were a miracle. Now the situation's changed.'

I imagined him as he was when a boy, pouring out water for us in Mahjoub's diwan. He used to perform such traditional tasks carelessly, saying neither 'yes' nor 'at your service', making you feel that you should be pouring the water yourself. I wondered whether, even at that early age, he knew that the fact that someone was older than someone else means nothing? His teachers at school used to say that he was a sly pupil, at the head of any movement of insubordination or trouble-making and yet escaping punishment: always it was he who committed the offence, while the punishment would be meted out to someone else. It was as though the fates were preparing him for this role. At the time of the wedding of Zein, Mahjoub entrusted him with providing fodder for the guests' donkeys, but he was more inclined towards providing liquor for those who liked to drink. When Mahjoub woke up to the fact that something was amiss, he found the donkeys without fodder and, on searching for Tureifi, discovered him drinking with the revellers. Mahjoub scolded him and slapped him; Tureifi didn't take it silently but shouted back at Mahjoub, saying: 'Who do you think you are?' and left the wedding and didn't participate in it. From his early youth he used to do things that weren't done: he would cross his legs in the presence of his elders, would yawn openly when Ali Wad Shayeb told one of his stories, and would elbow himself into the conversations of grown-ups and speak out his mind, always opposing or making fun of the opinions of men old enough to be his father. The consensus of opinion was that he was a good-for-nothing boy, and Mahjoub used to say to his father in company: 'May the Lord spare us the mischief of Tureifi your son.' Despite this, he always surprised people with his out-standing skill and proficiency in any activity he chose to take up. In the history of Wad Hamid he did several heroic things that had not earned sufficient appreciation from people, because no sooner had he done some laudable action than he would destroy it with an action that was disgraceful in people's eyes, as though doing so on purpose, as though not caring whether people thought he'd acted well or badly. They were at a loss about him, regarding him with a mixture of admiration and wariness.

'The people,' said Tureifi, 'want a leader who knows the nature of his role in the village. Mahjoub was making himself into a tribal sheikh — a lot of hullabaloo and nothing to show for it. I know Mahjoub's your close friend, but that's the truth.'

I remembered that in the great flood he had rescued Ammouna

bint at-Taum from drowning and that he'd stayed up all night swimming between the island and the shore, untying a cow here, setting up a barrier there, or lifting up something that had fallen down, and stretching out a helping hand to someone seeking aid. In the morning, when the people were collectively combating the floor, he was asleep at home. Reckoning up who'd been there and who hadn't, they said: 'Tureifi, the son of Bakri, may God frustrate him – on such a day everybody's busy and he's asleep on his back at home.'

Ammouna bint at-Taum told them otherwise, but they refused to believe her. When there was a gathering of people, Sa'eed Asha 'l-Baytat would say: 'I swear to you, Tureifi, the son of Bakri is a fine man, but you're blind to it.'

Ali Wad Shayeb would laugh with the rest of the scoffers, saying: 'Asha 'l-Baytat's making himself into a propaganda broadcasting station for the son of Bakri. It's a case of the blind and the halt.'

Despite this, they gathered one forenoon under the big sayyal tree in the centre of the village and elected him as their leader.

He continued his speech with, 'The question of kinship and friendship has nothing to do with it. The question's one of principles.'

'What's your principle?' I said to him.

He said pompously, as it appeared to me at the time, though I may have been mistaken, 'My principle is to extricate this village from the pit of backwardness and underdevelopment. We must keep up with progress. The age is one of science and technology.'

Then he looked at me challengingly and asked of me, 'And what's your position in what's happening?'

I laughed and my laughter annoyed him, and with, as it seemed to me, great pomposity, he said, 'It's a serious matter, not a joke. What's your position?'

It would have been easy in those particular circumstances to have made fun of him, but I resisted and kept quiet. Perhaps he did not realize why I had a soft spot for him, for he was Maryam's son and it was possible that he could have been my son had it not been for the fact that my grandfather had said no. She had supported her brother against him and had left her husband's house and stayed with Mahjoub, though Tureifi was her first-born son and she loved him very much and was proud of him. After that she never saw him again. Then she died in the month of Amsheer and we had buried her just before sunset. It was a painful occasion.

Tureifi was crying as I had never seen a human being cry and we had forcibly taken hold of him – Wad Rawwasi, Abdul Hafeez and I – to stop him entering the grave with her. Poor boy, he too suffered. Man, however ambitious he may be, is still the son of a woman. Perhaps he saw the reflections of those thoughts on my face, for he suddenly sat up straight and put out the cigarette he had in his hand. He stirred restlessly in his chair. He gave a muffled sigh and, lowering his head, examined the ground. Treating him gently, because of all I remembered, I asked him, 'Do you remember that dawn in Amsheer?'

'What dawn?' he said, raising his head in alarm.

'That memorable dawn,' I said to him, 'when the mosque, contrary to custom, was filled with worshippers – in Amsheer after we had buried your mother Maryam at night.'

He lowered his head, looking down at the ground and didn't answer.

'We carried you unconscious from the graveyard after the burial. Do you remember?'

'I don't remember,' he said sharply.

'You fainted at the graveside and woke to the weeping of the worshippers in the mosque at dawn. Between sleeping and wakefulness you had a dream. Do you remember?'

'I don't remember,' he said violently.

'You heard a voice,' I said to him.

'I heard no voice,' he said.

'Someone called out to you.'

'No one called out to me,' he said with irritation.

'Do you remember what happened that dawn?' I said to him. 'Do you remember the weeping of the worshippers? Do you remember that you wept till you almost passed out?'

Raising his head, he gathered his wits about him with an obvious effort, for he was shaken, and said in a trembling voice, 'I don't remember.'

Perhaps I was hard on him, but one of the reasons for my return was to learn the truth of the matter before it was too late, for I too had crossed that bridge and had buried well-loved things, and I had seen things sprout up in the same way as the graves will split open on the Day of Resurrection, and we must come to comprehend the connection between the two halves of the millstone. I said to him – and maybe I was being cruel – albeit unintentionally in those circumstances.

'I shall tell you what happened. A messenger came to you. You rose in a dazed state and walked behind him in the darkness and saw in front of you a fortress, and it was as if the darkness had been cleft open to reveal it. Its lights came and went. You followed the messenger and found yourself where there was noise and the sound of singing and dancing. There was a celebration being held in the midst of that darkness. Doors were opened and you walked through corridor after corridor till you arrived at a spacious hall with lamps and lanterns. In the middle of the place was one in the guise of two. The one welcomed you with smiles, and the two greeted you warmly. And the voice said to you: "Welcome to Tureifi, the son of Bakri. Welcome to the new leader of Wad Hamid." He seated you either on the right or the left and they brought you drink. You awoke and heard Asha l'-Baytat giving the call to the dawn prayer in a voice that stirred you and revived your longings and sorrows. You walked between the darkness and the light, not knowing in what time you were, yesterday, today or tomorrow, nor in what place, here or there. You met a great concourse of people who had gathered without reason or prior arrangement, as though they were expecting you. You remembered the people meeting at the grave just before sunset and the people under the large sayyal tree in the centre of the village at forenoon and you remembered a first forenoon, before you were born, or your father, or your grandfather were born by many, many generations. People were rushing about hither and thither, search-ing for something and for nothing, and you and Bandarshah were holding the threads of chaos, in the middle of it and above it. It was a feast. You wept with the people and the people wept with you. And the stranger by the window was appearing and disappearing. I asked, "Did you see the person who was there?" Some people said yes and you said no. Do you remember?'

We were silent for a long time and the surface of his face was like a sky whose clouds gather and disperse, then form anew. And I thought I would rescue him from drowning because he was Maryam's son, so I laughed and he too laughed as I had expected in such circumstances.

'And now I'll answer your question,' I said to him. 'My position is, as you can see, a complicated one.'

He had all but regained his composure. He looked at his watch and stood up to leave. I was struck by the similarity between him and Mahjoub: the way of standing and of sitting, the laughter, the expression in the eyes, the gestures. He had nothing of his mother. He had come to persuade me to join his camp. He had not succeeded but perhaps, like me, he had comprehended something.

As he walked towards the door, he said, 'I too will answer you. That dawn I saw a vision and I heard a voice, but it was not as you have described it.'

CHAPTER TWELVE

ASAB AR-RASOUL took the yoke off the bull's neck before the break of dawn by as much time as it would take to water six hauds of land. It was wintertime, in the month of Amsheer, as his son Mukhtar related years and years later. By the edge of the river bank was a fire of *talk* wood keeping him company in his loneliness and providing him with a certain amount of warmth. He was alone on the waterwheel, walking behind the lone bull, then running off to hold back the water from the haud of land that had been filled, and opening up its flow into an unwatered haud. There were few men about in those days. Mukhtar Wad Hasab ar-Rasoul says that his father released the bull from the waterwheel and led it to the pen not far away, and stood by the fire, looking at its sparse light reflected on the water. Suddenly he heard a movement in the water as though a crocodile had surfaced, and he looked and saw the light reflected from the burning fire undulating over the rippling waves. He looked again and saw a black shape moving towards him. Hasab ar-Rousal said, as he reported by his son Mukhtar: 'I saw the black shape spread between river and sky as though stretched out between the fire on the bank and the faint glow of dawn under the line of the horizon. I felt myself losing control, and as I was sinking I remembered that I had performed my ablutions for the morning prayer and that I was still in a state of purity. I began to surface as I clung desperately to the hems of the Koran, repeating the Holy Names mechanically, as an illiterate would. I unsheathed my weapons: Ya Sin, Ha Mim, Kaf Lam Mim, Qaf Sad 'Ain,[29] with each name pushing me upwards until I returned close to what I had been in my first state, while my heart leapt about and the sweat poured off me, and my despondency and distress was such that no one could know of it but God. I saw that the dark shape had become a solitary devil instead of a collection of devils, and I told myself that He who had protected me against their evil would also protect me against the evil of this one. I took courage and pulled myself together; swallowing hard, I said to the monster standing in the water between earth and sky, "Peace be upon him who has followed guidance."[30] He did not answer my greeting and continued to wade through the water, making his way towards where I was. I repeated "There is no god but God" and "God is great" several times, and between every "In the name of God" and "There is no power or strength except through God", I would feel that one of the angels of peace was alighting in my heart, so that I found what had been lost of my tongue and my courage. In that state I asked him – though I had no need to ask: "Are you devil or human?"

'He answered me, standing before me, and it was as if a hundred leagues lay between him and me. He said in Arabic but with a foreign accent, "Devil."

'My fears had become a single fear, and it was as though my ears that had been closed were all at once opened and I heard the sound of the waves on the bank like claps of thunder.

' "A devil coming from where?" I said to him.

' "Where devils come from," he said, both his fluency and his foreign accent becoming more apparent.

' "Where do devils come from?" I said to him.

' "From far away beyond the sea," he answered.

' "And what did you come here for?" I said to him.

' "Because I'm hungry," he said.

'Suddenly, as a cloud disperses so did my fear. I told myself that a hungry devil was something unacceptable to the human mind. Either he was a puny devil or he was a human being like you or me. I laughed and heard my laughter travel to the other bank and return. I said to him, having again become Hasab ar-Rasoul Wad Mukhtar and the world was Wad Hamid and the time was a dawn which was about to break, ' "A hungry devil? God keep you safe, you're a human being just like myself."

'He had come out of the water and I saw him unmistakably standing before me: white-skinned, tall of stature, with green eyes that I saw in the light of my fire. Nonetheless he was a human being just like you and me.

' "You fool," he said to me, "do devils appear floating about on the Nile? I'm a man, tired and hungry. For days and nights my eyes have not tasted sleep nor my stomach food."

' "Greetings," I said to him. "A thousand welcomes to the foreign guest who has come from God's lands. You have arrived at the place of someone who takes good care of his guests, a place where the tired can have a rest." Once again I was as I used to be and more – Hasab ar-Rasoul Wad Mukhtar the son of Hasab ar-Rasoul the gallant, the provider, the saviour of the orphan, the one whose fire does not go out and whose guest is never turned away. God knows, we were in a bad way; we had but a single nanny goat that was in milk and a lone bull without a cow. There wasn't a donkey or a saddle and our house was made of thatch as we hadn't yet built one of mud, and my son Mukhtar was at the breast. In the house there was a little millet but no ghee or meat. We'd planted wheat and were waiting for God's pleasure. Maymouna, Mukhtar's mother, made some porridge with a little milk and I set about eating at a slow pace so the guest should have his fill. In those days we didn't know about tea and coffee. We used to drink fenugreek and milk with dates and ghee but we had neither this nor that. The man ate greedily, while I gave thanks to God in a loud voice as though I'd eaten a whole calf, hoping that God would fill the rest of the guest's stomach. Though he belched, he said neither "Praise be to God" nor "Thanks be to God." I looked at his appearance: his face was like rock, his nose like that of a hawk, his teeth like those of a horse, the eyes green and shining like turquoise. How majestic is God's workmanship! His clothes were like those of Turkish soldiers, torn and tattered, wet and blood-stained. He had with him a tin, which I asked him about.

' "It contains the elixir," he said, laughing.

'I didn't talk with him much. After he'd eaten and drunk, I took him off to the mosque, which in those days was a single room of mud bounded by a straw fence. We were all related to one another, our houses being side by side. The men gathered in the mosque at forenoon to make the acquaintance of the stranger and everyone brought along what he could: some brought dates, some a little milk, others a few beans or some porridge. My uncle Mahmoud, being better off, slaughtered two chickens. We had lunch before lunchtime for our guest's sake. After lunch I told them the story and we began enquiring about who he was and the whys and the wherefores of him. My uncle Mahmoud opened the questioning by saying, ' "What's your name?"

'The stranger kept his head lowered for a long time in thought.

We exchanged glances, for it's a question that requires no thought. After a long time he said, ' "I don't know."

' "Is there any man who doesn't have a name?" my uncle Mahmoud asked him, greatly astonished – as indeed were we all.

' "I certainly had a name," said the man. "Bahloul. Bahdour. Shah. Khan. Mirza. Mirhan – I don't know."

'The names of jinn, I told myself – not sanctified by God.

' "Are you Moslem, Christian or Jewish?" I asked him.

'Once again he bent over in thought. After a while he said, "I' must have had a religion. I don't know."

'Abdul Khalik Wad Hamad, who was always the quickest of us to anger, asked him irritably, ' "O son of Adam, is there a human being who has no religion? You could be a fire-worshipper or a cow-worshipper or a worshipper of ashes. Tell us."

'I laughed and said to them, ' "Have we established that he's a human being? Isn't it possible that he could be a devil?"

'Rahmatallah Was al-Kashif also laughed and said, "Everything's possible in such times."

'We exchanged glances, while I felt that I was personally responsible for his being there. The man was silent, making no answer.

' "Do you remember where you came from?" I asked him.

'He answered immediately, "Caucas, Ahwaz. Khorassan, Azerbaijan, Isphahan, Samarkand, Tashkent. I don't know. From some faraway place. I was tired, hungry and ill."

'I remembered how he had looked at me from the water, like a ghoul, and I told myself that, having eaten his fill, he had no doubt gone back to being the devil he had been. Rahmatallah stole the question from the tip of my tongue.

' "Listen, you creature," he said to the man angrily. "Let's get things straight: are you human or a devil?"

'The man didn't hesitate, didn't think it over. He answered immediately, shooting a glance with his green eyes at Wad al-Kashif that almost drove him out of his mind.

' "Human. A son of Adam like yourselves."

'My uncle Mahmoud laughed – he was the most sensible of us, the most understanding, our sheikh and our leader.

' "Thanks be to God," he said, "so long as you know you are a human."

'Miftah al-Khazna Wad Abdul Maula was sitting far off by the door as usual so that if things got difficult he could make his

63

escape easily. He wouldn't ask any questions. If people laughed he would join in and if they were annoyed he would shut up. He moved close up to the man and said hesitantly, ' "Your Honour must needs remember something, anything. Rack your brains well, maybe God will bring something to mind."

' "Miftah al-Khazna right away called the man Your Honour," said Abdul Khalek, "Because he's white and his green eyes."

' "The man's a Turk without a doubt," Miftah al-Khazna answered him apprehensively. "He could be a sanjak or a sirdar or a hikamdar. We must watch out and be careful."

'My uncle Mahmoud laughed and said to him, ' "You're always scared about things, Wad Abdul Maula. Just for now we're interested in his name, his race and his religion. His rank is something we're not concerned with."

'Suddenly it was as if the man had woken up out of a trance, or as if he had seen a ghost. Fear showed on his face and he stood up to his full height and spread out his hands in the air as though thrusting off some danger that was walking towards him. Sparks flew from his eyes, anger and panic appeared on his face as he called out at the top of his voice, "Jang, Jang"[31] – and he spoke in some language we did not understand. Then, gripping his right side and letting out a great scream of pain, he fell down in a faint. When we examined him, we found a large wound the size of a hand's span under his ribs, with pus that had collected over two or three weeks. At first we reckoned that it was all up with him, then his breast began to rise and fall and sweat to break out on his face. All the time we had been putting questions to him, the man had been fatally wounded and we hadn't realized. We told ourselves that he must be a deserter from the Turkish army, but in those days we didn't have any news of battles having taken place up country. We brought him a bed to the mosque and nursed him for a whole month, telling ourselves that our friend would die today or the next day. The person who exerted herself most in tending him was Fatima the daughter of my uncle Jabr ad-Dar. She was the youngest of her sisters: Maryam the mother of Hajj Ahmed, Haleema the mother of Hamad, and Maymouna the mother of my son Mukhtar. Fatima was a young girl and hadn't reached maturity; she was the least beautiful of her sisters and was as thin as a grasshopper, yet she was worth ten men and had a mind sharp like a knife and a heart like a rock. I think she was the only girl, up river and down, who knew the Koran by heart;

she had learnt it with the boys in Hajj Saad's Koranic school, when she would recite it in a voice that was like the cooing of ring-doves. He's a liar the boy who tells you he beat her at running, swimming or climbing the date palms – until her father forbade her. She was a real devil. She didn't possess the bashfulness of women: her eyes were large and black, filling her whole face, and when you looked at her she would return your gaze till you, the man, lowered yours. What a girl! She would ride a donkey astride, like a man, and sow and plough as though she were a man. Her father always used to say, "God Almighty, may He be glorified, has given me four daughters – Haleema, Maryam, Maymouna and Allah Leena"[32] – Allah Leena being his son Rajab who gained the nickname by reason of his being so timorous – "and He blessed me with one son, Fatima." She exerted herself to the full in looking after the stranger. We would laugh at her and say, "That man may well be an afreet and not a human. Be careful he doesn't carry you off or make the ground swallow you up or do something terrible to you," to which she would say, "If he's a devil, I'm Iblis himself, chief of the devils." God's power be glorified, it was as if the man was not in actual fact human, for the illness he had would have killed an ox. After a month, while we were assembled in the mosque at forenoon, he opened his eyes. He looked at us for a while and said, ' "Who are you?"

' "We're the jinn who were with King Solomon," said Abdul Khalek with a laugh.

' "Where's this place?" said the man, turning to right and left.

' "This place is red-hot Hell," Wad Hamad said to him.

'As though trying hard to remember, the man looked up and down.

' "What brought me here?" he said.

' "The Ababeel Birds brought you."[33]

'The man jumped up, while we remained silent, watching him. He looked into our faces and paced backwards and forwards, then sat down on the low bed. Standing up again, he scrutinized his fingers and toes, and examined the rough cotton gown we'd dressed him in. Afterwards he sat down on the bed and was silent for a while.

' "What am I? Who am I?" he said.

'At that moment we all laughed and my uncle Mahmoud said to him, ' "Who are you? – that's the question."

'We found that he had indeed forgotten everything: his having come out of the Nile, the millet porridge he'd eaten in our house, and our having sat with him in the mosque. It was amazing; it was as though the man had been born anew that forenoon in the mosque. Before that he didn't remember a thing. We were puzzled and turned over in our minds what to do with him, then we asked him if he knew where he wanted to go, to which he answered that he knew of no place he wanted to go. We gave some thought as to what we should do about him. Should we throw him back into the Nile whence he had come? But the pity in our hearts overcame the feeling of caution, for we are a people who, despite our meagre resources, do not turn away somebody who seeks our help.

' "O servant of God," my uncle Mahmoud said to him, "we live, as you can see, under the protection of the Almighty. Our life is one of toil and austerity, but our hearts are filled with contentment and we accept the share that God has given us. We perform the prayers as laid down, we safeguard our honour, and we stand up to the vicissitudes of time and the batterings of fate. Having much does not make us arrogant; having little does not make us uneasy. The path that our life takes is drawn and known from cradle to grave. The little that we have we have achieved by the strength of our muscles; we have not violated the rights of any man or eaten from usury or ill-gotten gains. Peaceful people in times of peace, angry people in times of anger. Those who don't know us think we're weak, that a breath of wind would carry us off, yet in actual fact we are like the haraz trees that grow in the fields. And you, O servant of God, have come to us from we know not where; like God's ordinance and destiny the waves have cast you up at our doors, and we don't know who you are or where you're bound for, someone bent on good or bent on evil. At any event, we have accepted you in our midst in the same way as we accept the heat and the cold, death and life. You can live with us, having what we have and taking upon yourself what we take; if you're good, you'll find all goodness with us, and if you're evil, then God will be our protector and guardian."

'The man's eyes filled with tears and he went on repeating, ' "Yes. Yes. Yes."

'We also were greatly affected by my uncle Mahmoud's words in explaining our state of affairs and circumstances, as though he had been reading the page of the unknown from a book. After that we told ourselves that we should give him a name, for the man had no name. We therefore left my uncle Mahmoud to do the choosing. It was as though the name had been right there, awaiting its owner. Immediately my uncle Mahmoud said, ' "Dau al-Beit[34] – a blessed name. Perhaps the man came upon us in this way to bring us blessings and prosperity."

'We all agreed and said that, with God's blessing, Dau al-Beit it should be, and we all asked him laughing, what his name was and he answered happily, "Dau al-Beit."

'How magnificent is God's power! The moment he uttered the name he became something real, as though he had been just that from the very beginning. We looked at our friend and found that he was in truth Dau al-Beit – not Jabr ad-Dar or Miftah al-Khazna or Abdul Maula or Abdul Khalek, but Dau al-Beit. It was as though the name had been existing since time began, as something deposited with us in trust awaiting its owner, who came hastening from over the sea, from behind the unseen, to receive that which was held in trust for him. The Lord be praised!

'I looked at my friend and recollected my meeting with him only a month ago between the light and the darkness, as though he were a monster spread out between earth and sky, and suddenly he had never been any such thing. My little friend had contracted, grown smaller, had become Dau al-Beit, the poor stranger, a son of Adam who eats and drinks and laughs and cries and is born and dies, a human being just like you and me. I remembered my fear that dawn and I looked at my little friend and I laughed. How magnificent is God's power!

'After that we came to the question of religion. My uncle Mahmoud said to him, "Dau al-Beit, we are Moslems, but we are not fanatical on the question of religion. Every soul has what it has gained and God is He who chooses amongst His servants. If we had known you had a faith, we would have left you in your faith. However, since you do not know what religion you are, what do you think about us taking you with us into the faith of Islam? We shall earn merit and you will escape from God's wrath, also it will help you in your dealings with the people of the village if you want to get married and settle down."

'Dau al-Beit accepted straight away, so my uncle Mahmoud taught him the two doctrinal formulas, which he repeated in a clear voice that made our hearts thump and our eyes water, especially Miftah al-Khazna, who was overcome by a state of rapture that affected us all, and who went on repeating, "I bear witness that there is no god but God and I bear witness that Mohammed is the Messenger of God" over and over again, as though it were he who had entered Islam and not the stranger. In truth we were all of us in an extraordinary state that forenoon in the mosque; it was as if we were witnessing a miracle. We were certain that the waves of the Nile had thrown up Dau al-Beit on to the shore of Wad Hamid so that he might be for us a harbinger of blessings and good fortune. It was Abdul Khalek Wad Hamad who brought us out of our trance by raising his voice amidst the people who, weeping and tearful, were uttering God's praises.

' "Friends, say a prayer for the Prophet, and listen here: we're making a big hullabaloo but shouldn't we first make sure whether the man's circumcised or not?" We examined Dah al-Beit and found that he was, alas, uncircumcised. Nevertheless, our joy at his entering Islam was not diminished and we made up our minds to have him circumcised at a big feast with music and singing and religious chanting after the wheat harvest. The fact was that that season there had been no circumcision or wedding, and we told ourselves that it would be a celebration the like of which had not previously taken place in the village, because Wad Hamid has been wholly Moslem ever since God created it and we'd never seen anyone newly adopting the faith of Islam. And thus we would rejoice and be happy, singing and dancing and eating and drinking; the celebration would be a conglomeration of celebrations; a naming celebration, a circumcision celebration and a religious celebration.

'God's Omnipotence so wanted it that the celebration should be all of that as well as a celebration of marriage, because Dau al-Beit had at one fell swoop entered into our life as though he were one of us. Each one of us invited him to work in his field, but he refused, saying, "Give me a piece of land to work myself, for I'm a stranger and I don't want to enter into disputes with the inhabitants of the village because of problems over work." My uncle Mahmoud said, "By God, Dau al-Beit's a sensible man." He himself had a piece of land that had been left uncultivated since time immemorial, measuring half a feddan.[35] He said to him, "It's difficult to produce anything from this piece of land, but if you want it, you can have it as a gift from me." Dau al-Beit accepted the gift and began work immediately. Each one of us helped as much as we could. He had brought with him some tobacco plant seed in the tin he'd had with him when he'd emerged from the

Nile and which he called the elixir. How magnificent is God's power! He worked like a demon descended from Iblis himself, never slackening or tiring night and day. You would never find him lying down or sitting, always standing straight up or bent over his hoe and mattock, his hands seemingly possessed of magic. He cultivated tomatoes, onions, okra, wheat, barley and beans; there wasn't a single thing he didn't do. After three months he was reaping his wheat at the very same time as ourselves, though we had planted ours a full month before him. Whenever I would see him working in the heat of the day while people were taking a rest at siesta time, or at night when the cold was sharp as a knife, I'd look and marvel and say to myself, "I wonder, is he a human in the shape of a devil or a devil in the shape of a human?"

'As we were preparing for the celebration I mentioned, Dau al-Beit broached the subject of marriage. We were all gathered in the mosque after Friday prayers when he opened the subject.

' "Friends," he said, "you've done me a favour I'll never forget as long as I live, but there's no point in saying more because it's all known and understood. I am now, thanks be to God, one of you, as though I had been with you from of old. In a word, I want from you a favour bigger than all those of the past: I want from you relationship and kinship in accordance with the law of God and His Prophet."

'We were struck completely speechless, each one of us thinking the same thoughts. Our brother in Islam, attending the five prayers with us — that was true; we'd given him a name, we shared our farming and our drudgery with him — that was true; he worked like an army of men — that was true; he had, during his short stay with us, won our affection as though he had been with us from of old — that was true; but to marry off one of our daughters to him when we knew next to nothing about him, and his eyes were green and ours were black, his face as white as cotton, ours like tanned hide; to marry off one of our daughters to him who had emerged from the water, while we had come from clay; to him who had been a Moslem for six months, while we had been Moslems from time immemorial; to him who, while our life begins and ends between the Nile below and the desert above, has his life beginning we know not how or ending we know not how; to him whose name emerged when he emerged, while our names are interlinked, handed down from father to son, like a structure

69

that is tightly fitted together, one name on top of another, right up to Adam – that was quite another matter.

'After a while my uncle Mahmoud raised his head and turned his gaze upon us, looking at us one by one as though reading our thoughts. He was a great man, may God show him abounding mercy, one of our worthy forefathers the like of which time will never again bestow. When his eyes met those of my uncle Jabr ad-Dar, his cousin, he kept on for a while looking at him, till Jabr ad-Dar lowered his gaze and averted his face. I avow my belief in God, the people were as quiet as could be, each one of them concerned with things deep inside himself. I too found myself in a state of great turmoil and, in God's truth, at that moment I heartily regretted having taken Dau al-Beit from the Nile. I told myself: I wish I'd let him be so that he could go his own sweet way. I glanced at my uncle Jabr ad-Dar, his head bowed, and I felt sad at what would happen. However, my uncle Mahmoud decided the question and put a stop to all doubt. Turning towards us, he said, ' "When we first took Dau al-Beit as our brother here in this place, and said to him: You have the same rights and the same obligations as ourselves, we were talking as men, not as children, talk that was serious and not joking. Brotherhood is one, not two, just as religion is one, not two. There's not one religion for life and another religion for death, and there's no friendship in work and yet not in marriage. Dau al-Beit has become just like us, for better or for worse, in good times and in bad. Seeing that he has asked to be related to us through marriage in accordance with the law of God and His Prophet, then he's very welcome. Had I a daughter, I would gladly give her to him in marriage."

'Silence – I avow my belief in God – it was as if you could hear the blood coursing through the veins as a state of bewilderment took possession of me, my mind going and coming, not knowing whether what had happened in the mosque that day was good or evil. Our affairs had been going along a set line. Then, we knew not how, we found ourselves on a path, leading we knew not where. I glanced at my uncle, Jabr ad-Dar, who was frowning as though the words were addressed solely to him. Suddenly Miftah al-Khazna called out at the top of his voice, "God is great. God is great," and Dau al-Beit the stranger burst into tears. God be glorified, he was like a mother who loses her only son. Miftah al-Khazna joined him for he was naturally always on the brink of tears, sometimes calling out "God is great", at others "Spread the good tidings". Then Timsah Wad Hasan, Wad Bekheit, Wad Suleiman, Wad al-Khashif, Wad Hamad, and finally Jabr ad-Dar as well, joined in the weeping. Something was found and something was lost to us that day. We didn't know why or for what we were weeping, whether it was for what we had gained or for what had been lost. My uncle Mahmoud was not a man who cried easily, but his eyes were bathed in tears, while I was confused, not knowing whether to be happy or sad, saying to myself, "Praise be to God, is this a funeral or a wedding?" We were seized by a frenzy of yearning an ecstasy of love, as though we wee at some Sufi gathering for the invocation of the Lord's name, while Dau al–Beit the stranger sat in the middle, connected with all that was taking place, and Miftah al-Khazna was calling out at the top of his voice, "Spread the good tidings. Spread the good tidings." '

CHAPTER THIRTEEN

T HE village woke early to the women's cries of joy in Mahmoud's house and in that of his cousin and son-in-law,
Jabr ad-Dar. The men had performed the dawn prayer in
community and had remained on, waiting. At sunrise the calf had
been slaughtered in the mosque courtyard and Mahmoud led Dau
al-Beit off by the arm and made him step over the slaughtered
calf, while Miftah al-Khazna called out, 'Spread the good tidings.
Spread the good tidings.' On that day Dau al-Beit was like a king
among his subjects, wearing a green silk kaftan, a red skull-cap
and large white turban, and enveloped in a red-fringed shawl; his
shoes were red and shone in the light. People, looking at the way
he was *got up*, would laugh joyfully, for among them were some
who were wearing only rags round their waists, while others had
clothes that were filthy or in tatters. They also laughed happily
when Dau al-Beit renewed his acceptance of Islam and recited
some verses from the Chapter of the Forenoon that Fatima the
daughter of Jabr ad-Dar had taught him, pronouncing the letter
dad and the letter jim as though they were dal, and they went on
exclaiming 'There is no god but God' and 'God is great'. Then
Abdul Khalek Wad Hamad stood up and said, 'In the name of
God, the Merciful, the Compassionate, and it is through His power
and strength that we have named this newborn child Dau al-Beit',
this being their custom when they gave a name to a child, and
Dau al-Beit laughed like a child and they all laughed merrily. It
was as though the child had been born at sunrise and had matured
into a boy ready for circumcision by forenoon. They seated him
on the large bowl made of haraz wood turned upside down, with
Mahmoud holding him on the right and Abdul Khalek on the
left. Rahmatallah Wad al-Kashif honed his knife and in an instant
the blood was flowing and the matter was over and done with, as
Miftah al-Khazna jogged up and down and shouted out the good

news and the men laughed in joy and wonder as they had never laughed before. The women in the mud and straw huts scattered around the mosque heard the uproar made by the man and broke into trilling cries of joy.

It was as though the child, born at sunrise and circumcised at forenoon, was ready for marriage after the afternoon prayer. It was a memorable marriage and was attended by all the neighbours of Wad Hamid, people coming from the other river bank and from the villages scattered along both banks. At that period of time there were few people about and they lived in widely separated villages, their faint lights appearing as though suspended in the sky, while the voices travelled from bank to bank, so weak that they were scarcely discernible to the ear. Yet people knew what was taking place across the river as though there were invisible bridges between the two banks; they knew who was watering his field by night and who by day, who'd fallen ill and who'd been born and who'd died and who'd been married, and who'd sold and who'd bought. They were united by bonds of kinship and relationship through marriage, while markets and business dealings brought them together for the bartering of seeds for planting and date palm seedlings and studs for cows and donkeys, and the religious chanters and the singers and the Koran reciters all brought them together. Their way of life was the same from where the two rivers met to beyond the frontiers of Egypt. There was nothing extraordinary, therefore, about the fact that word got round concerning the big celebration in Wad Hamid so that they came from up river and down, from north and south of the valley, by boat across the river, by donkey and on foot, bearing their presents: dates and corn and barley and beans and onions and ghee and oil. Each one brought according to his means: this one bringing a cock, that one a lamb or a young goat, coming as dispersed as drizzle, then quickly joining and coalescing into a vast ocean that raged and swelled with a new life that was bigger than the sum of its parts.

Dau al–Beit was the focus on that day at the height of summer. A woman reaches the edge of the quarter with the sweat pouring from her, for she has set out from her home at daybreak and has arrived when the sun is at its zenith; she hears the sounds of rejoicing and inhales the smells of the feast, and she is infected by the well-being of the large gathering of people who have planted the banner of life amidst that nothingness, and from afar she gives vent to trilling cries of joy, primarily to express her sheer happiness at being alive, but also by way of announcing to the crowd that she too is here and that she possesses a voice that can express all that. Her voice joins the tumult adding to it a musical note that the ear does not immediately distinguish right away, but listening carefully realizes it is there and that the voice of the totality would not be complete without it. They arrive by ones and twos, thin and emaciated, every back bowed, every shoulder weighed down by the burdens of life and death, and the great concourse takes them over so that each one becomes himself and something more. Today the wise man will behave foolishly, the religious man will get drunk, and the sober will dance; a man will look at his wife in the circle of dancers as though he is seeing her for the first time; there is nothing wrong with that, for they are confirming life's force amidst all that nothingness. From time to time a group will arrive racing each other on their donkeys in a cloud of fine sand and dust, as though they are a whirlwind breathed out by the desert, a whirlwind that does not die but enters the throng which boils and surges. They come like grains of wheat in a heap of wheat, each grain autonomous, holding within itself a great secret. Occasionally a man will arrive on a donkey with a saddle and bit, well turned out and smartly dressed, and the donkey will announce its owner's arrival. They come, all of them poor in varying degrees, and are encompassed by a harmonious orbit rotating round its axis at a predestined rate. They come weak and return strong, needy and return rich, astray and find right guidance. Today the parts will be united and each one will become the one.

It is thus no wonder that that infection flowed in Jabr ad-Dar's soul and made him forget, now in the height of summer, that bitterness that had afflicted him more than a year ago in the depth of winter. The times now are joyful, life is good and the moon is full, and voices, well-ordered and interlocked, are telling you that death is nothing more than one of life's meanings. He stood up and addressed the people after the marriage, saying that they all knew that his daughter Fatima was as precious to him as his hearing and sight. God had willed that Dau al-Beit, of all people should have her. He said that at first he had not agreed, but that today he was the happiest of men.

On that day in Amsheer, Jabr ad-Dar had left the mosque sad and worried. He had performed the night prayer alone in his house and his daughter had come to read the Koran to him as was her habit every night. The verses were not sad but they filled him with sorrow. In this state of mind, he had asked her for her opinion of Dau al–Beit, to which she had answered him, 'All right – there's nothing wrong with him.'

'I see that you talk a lot with him in the fields,' he said to her gently.

'I teach him reading and writing and learning the Koran by heart.'

'I dare say he learns well.'

'He memorizes quickly, as though remembering things he'd known long ago.'

'Does he mention anything of his past?' he asked her.

'Vague memories come to him. Mostly memories of battles and wars. He talks of stabbing and striking, of cannons and gunpowder. He sweats and when the sweat dries, he is overcome by trembling; he almost loses consciousness. Then he regains his normal condition, and he laughs and I laugh.'

Jabr ad–Dar rose from the pelt he used as a prayer-mat and sat on the low bed. He seated her beside him and put his arm around her.

'Many times it's as if he remembers his mother,' she said sadly. 'He always says words like Mama, Ama. His eyes fill with tears. He jabbers away in a strange tongue. When he comes to and I ask him about it, he says he doesn't remember. Poor thing.'

Jabr ad–Dar lowered his head in silence for a time, while his hand tenderly caressed his daughter's cheek. Suddenly he asked her, 'If he asked you to marry him, would you accept him?'

She was silent for a while, then she laughed and didn't answer.

At this he related to her what had occurred in the mosque, then he said, 'Mahmoud was talking and looking at me as though his words were meant for me rather than anyone else. I have no daughter to give in marriage but you. Whether you say yes or no, the matter rests in your hands.'

While they were so engaged, Mahmoud entered. He greeted them and sat down. Then, directing his words to the girl and ignoring the father, he said, 'Fatima, Dau al–Beit wants to get married. He broached the subject with us after the prayers. When the people had gone I asked him if he had anyone particular in mind. He said "I want Fatima the daughter of Jabr ad–Dar." Do you accept him?'

She did not hesitate or think; right away she said in a low but clear and decisive voice, 'Yes'.

Jabr ad-Dar remembered that as he stood making a speech in the mosque after the marriage contract ceremony. He said that he didn't at first agree but today he was the happiest of men and that he had waived everything and asked for no dowry for his daughter, neither to be paid in advance nor in the eventuality of divorce.

The people cried out, 'Spread the good tidings. Spread the good tidings'. They waved their hands and brandished their sticks, shook each other by the hand and embraced, and the trilling cries of joy from the women surged and gushed forth, echoing in and around the mosque. They were carried by the winds of summer, which circulated them in the courtyards the alleyways, the fields, above the tops of the date palms, the acacia, the sant, the haraz and sayyal trees, above the esparto and the tamarisk and the ushar bushes, and across the Nile. The reverberations came back magnified from the ends of the village to their source where the drums droned and thundered and the people formed circle within circle round the dancers and singers and religious chanters. Then the sun sank and the full moon mounted her throne and the world was filled with bliss; time was untroubled, happiness and joy complete, while the fires of the quarter were lit, and the dance circle at the large sayyal tree in the centre of the village swirled with people. The sounds of great rejoicing broke out from the feet of the dancers, from the palms of those clapping in time, and from the throats of the singers, from the drums and the tambouras, from the roofs of the houses and from the spaces between the huts, from the courtyards and open spaces and alleyways, and from the places where the animals were tethered. Tonight every old man is young, every young man is infatuated with love, every woman truly feminine, every man an Abu Zeid al-Hilali.[36] Tonight everything is alive. Fragrance is diffused, happiness complete, light radiates, and the armies of grief have taken to flight. Every limb walks with a swinging gait, every breast trembles, every buttock quivers, every eye is darkened with kohl, every cheek is smooth, every mouth is honeyed, every waist slim, every action beautiful – and all the people are Dau al-Beit. He was standing in the centre of the circle brandishing a whip of hippopotamus hide above the women dancers, while the men sprang one after another into the circle to vie with one another, and he would strike about him as he pleased. Abdul Khalek Wad Hamad, the dauntless champion, entered the circle, bared his back and stood firm to receive the lashes. At once Hasab al-Rasoul Wad Mukhtar, his rival and peer, came out to join him, and Dau al-Beit began wielding his whip, bringing it down once on Abdul Khalek's back and once on Hasab ar-Rasoul's. As each whiplash landed, the women let out trilling cries of joy and the men shouted happily. The roaring of the drums grew louder, breaking up and reassembling round Dau al-Beit as he stood at the centre of the hubbub, his whip raised above everybody, appearing and disappearing among the crush, as though there and yet not there.

He passed like a dream, as though he had never been, yet he left behind him his son Isa, who later came to be known as Bandarshah. He was born three months after his death, black of face like his mother, his eyes green like those of his father: a person apart, resembling neither this nor that.

CHAPTER FOURTEEN

THIS is what Abdul Khalek said, as narrated by his son Hamad Wad Haleema, years and years later.

'My uncle Mahmoud, Hasab ar-Rasoul, Dau al-Beit and I were on the river bank dismantling the waterwheel. It was the time of the flooding and the river was overflowing its banks, giving warning of danger, becoming higher as it were, in strides; you felt the rise of it every moment. The sun had just set, changing the river into a sea of blood. The three of us were down below, with Dau al-Beit above on the edge of the bank, and we were handing him up the pieces of wood for him to pull on to firm ground. Suddenly, the earth under our feet collapsed, and before we knew it, the three of us were out in the river, wrestling against the waves, and in a matter of moments we were scattered to right and left. My uncle Mahmoud and I were Nile crocodiles; as for Hasab ar-Rasoul, he was a champion of things on land, no one getting the better of him at running, wrestling, wielding a whip, dancing and clapping in time, but in the river he was no use at all. From afar we saw him sinking and surfacing, and we began battling against the current in an effort to reach him. It was hopeless; the current was overpowering, supreme, as it buffeted us. I stretched out my hand to him, and he stretched out his towards me, but it was to no avail. My uncle Mahmoud was circling and twisting in the water like a crazed crocodile, trying to find a breach in the sea of water so as to break through to Hasab ar-Rasoul. I caught a glimpse of him in the redness of dusk and it was as if he had reconciled himself to death. I heard him call out, "Save yourselves or we're all lost. God be with you. Look after Maymouna, Mukhtar and the little ones. Goodbye. Goodbye."

'While in this situation I saw Dau al-Beit striking about in the waves, making in our direction. My uncle Mahmoud had disappeared and there was no sign of him, while I was sinking and floating up to the surface with the waves slapping me in the face like the force of God. As I plunged down into the depths, I saw Dau al-Beit, as though suspended by the threads of the setting sun, lifting Hasab ar-Rasoul high up in his arms in the redness of the dusk. Then I saw the date palms and the other trees on the two banks as though they were plunging down with me, and the whole universe was coloured with the hue of blood. After that I remember nothing except finding myself on the bank among the throng of people, with voices battling together and phantom shapes leaping up here and there. I looked and saw Hasab ar-Rasoul stretched out, as though dead, and I heard my uncle Mahmoud's voice calling out "Dau al-Beit, Dau al-Beit". All of a sudden Hasab ar-Rasoul got to his feet and began running about, looking into people's faces and calling out "Dau al-Beit, Dau al-Beit". After that the people got into a state of extreme agitation and excitement; some of them went down to the water, some ran along the bank; torches were lit and people called out from place to place and from bank to bank, until the whole world was calling out in the depths of darkness "Dau al-Beit, Dau al-Beit". We waited day after day between despair and expectancy, saying to ourselves that maybe there was still hope. But Dau al-Beit had disappeared without trace; he had gone whence he had come, from water to water, from darkness to darkness, with Hasab ar-Rasoul weeping and saying, "It can't be, it can't be."

'We mourned for him as though we had lost the boon of hearing and of sight. He had lived among us like a spirit and had departed like a dream; for not more than ten harvests it had been – five years by the count of years – during which he had accomplished more than other people accomplish in a lifetime. The good things of the world rained down upon him as though he had only to say "Be" and it was. He would plant winter crops both in summer and winter and would work the whole year round, untiringly and without letting up. He brought date seedlings of every sort and kind from the lands of the Mahas, right up to the country of the Rubatab, and he taught the earth to grow tobacco and he taught us to grow oranges and bananas. We, between one harvest and another, take a rest, but he would travel with the camel caravans, one time to the lands of the Kababeesh, another to Berber or Suakim, and sometimes to the borders of Egypt, and would return bearing clothes and perfumes and all sorts of table utensils and things to eat and drink which we had never known before in Wad Hamid. He grew in stature, and we with him, as though the Lord, may He be glorified, had sent him to us to invigorate our lives, and then go on his way. We built houses of mud instead of straw, and he who had only one room made himself three, and he who didn't have a courtyard made himself one. We rebuilt the mosque, enlarging it and spreading it with carpets and rugs, a present from Dau al-Beit. He built himself, high on the hill, a citadel, houses within houses and diwans within diwans and courtyards within courtyards. Praise be to God, you would see it from afar as though it were a city all on its own, when previously it had been abandoned wasteland on the outskirts of the village. Fatima, the daughter of Jabr ad-Dar wept copious tears for him, like a she-camel whose young has been separated from her.

'We used to recall together what had happened at sunset that day. My uncle Mahmoud said that he remembers catching a glimpse of Dau al-Beit as though suspended between sky and earth, surrounded by a green glow. After that he remembers nothing except finding himself on the river's bank as though having woken from a dream, with the people shouting at one another and running hither and thither. Hasab ar-Rasoul said that he remembers, while between death and life, that he saw Dau al-Beit as in the heart of the red dusk, moving ever further away. Suddenly a giant's hand had stretched out from the redness of the dusk and had snatched him up and cast him away so that he found himself on the bank. He woke up and found that the world was darkness and that everyone was shouting "Dau al-Beit."

'Hasab ar-Rasoul's eyes fill with tears as he says, "God have mercy on Dau al-Beit. He paid with his life for the porridge he ate with us the first day. He passed away like a dream, as though he had never been – were it not for his son Isa who was born three months after his death. We look at his face but we do not see Dau al-Beit; we look at his eyes and we see the exact replica of Dau al-Beit."

BOOK TWO

MERYOUD

CHAPTER ONE

H E FILLED his chest with air and let his face be bathed by the dawn breeze; but that did nothing to raise his spirits. He took his time before descending into the out-stretched, flattened land, with the date groves behind it, and behind that the river appearing here and there between the gaps in the trees.

The scene assumed a particular poignancy as though Meheimeed was looking at it for the last time. His face was tense as if he was resisting an overpowering desire to cry.

Look to the right. Over there. Where is the thick forest of talh acacia in which they would play during the days of childhood? The smell of the talh flowers, especially at the time of the flood. And there, by the bend in the path, opposite the large canal, the huge densely leafed haraz tree proudly rose, its yellow fruit glittering like golden earrings. That water had another taste. That water-jar, without a covering, from which every passer-by drank, had its dried gourd that swung above the water, striking to left and right. Who had set it up? No one remembers. But it did not lack someone to fill it up morning and evening. The taste of tanned leather, the taste of the water in the waterskin hanging from the beams on his grandfather's verandah. The taste of the Nile water at the time of the flood. The taste of water-soaked wood, of leaves, of mud. The taste of death. Clear in the sandy places, turbid in the muddy parts. The whole of the sap of life in Wad Hamid.

Tightening his grip on the ivory handle of the ebony stick, he pushed on with a resolve that would weaken and then grow strong. How strange this stick was now: like a naked woman among men. He is conscious of its touch, and he remembers Maryam. That voice. That time of youth. That dream.

Every day at dawn he leaves his house and takes this path to the river. He swims and returns at the rising of the sun. He tries to awaken the slumbering ghosts in his soul. Sometimes luck comes his way and he hears and sees. The visions and voices spring from under his feet with the tapping of his stick on the path. Here is where the thresher was at harvest time. The smell of straw. The smell of wheat. The smell of cowpats. The smell of milk when it has just been drawn off. The smell of mint. The smell of limes.

Mahjoub, Abdul Hafeez, Taher, Sa'eed and himself. He closes his eyes, he sees them as they were. Ever on the move, running, jumping, shinning up trees and jumping down from the branches and rolling in the sand, living like water and air. He taps with his stick against the trunk of a tree. He hears his grandfather's laughter. He sees his face clearly. The small, deeply set eyes. The slightly jutting chin. The prominent forehead. The emaciated cheeks. The small mouth. The thin lips. A black face, as smoothly black as velvet, and the eyes that become blue and green and red according to circumstances and situations.

He never imagines him on his own. Always he sees him in a group: on his right Mukhtar Wad Hasab ar-Rasoul, and on his left Hamad Wad Haleena, with him in the middle of the group. He remembers him now with a mixture of sadness and malice. Passing over all his sons, he had chosen him to be his shadow on earth; he had left him the house, the prayer mat made of leopard skins, the brass ewer, and the string of prayer beads made from sandalwood, and this stick. What does the mirror reflect now?

He had crossed the highway leading to the souk. He saw the date palm at the intersection of the paths and, without thinking, headed for it. He sank down in exhaustion by it and rested himself against the trunk.

They were like twin brothers; it was as though the two of them had divided up equally between them the sum of their ages: he was no younger than his grandfather, the grandfather no older than his grandson. How strange that was! When racing, they would arrive together, shoulder to shoulder. Together they would set traps for birds, would fish, would vie in climbing the most difficult of the date palms. Wrestling together, one day one of them would win, the next he'd be the loser. Together they'd enter the dance circle and no dancer or clapper could compete with them; the dancer would move between grandfather and grandson in a field of destructive, magnetic gravitation. The circle would grow more dense, the clapping louder and the dancer would sway about, as though tied by unseen strings, between the two poles of the compass, tossing her perfumed hair once against the face of the past, once against the face of the future. They would share out the spoils between them: no victor and no vanquished. Their eyes would glitter, they would yell, would fly through the air and land like two predatory eagles. What a strange sight it was!

Yet that morning the grandson had gone further, and perhaps at that instant the grandfather's voice, as Meheimeed now recalled, was not devoid of a ring of envy. He had felt for him then a bitter hatred: had the boat collapsed with them and he were drowning, the grandson at that moment would not have stretched out a helping hand to him. He had followed in his tracks, step by step, had become like him until finally they were as alike as an odd shoe to its pair. An idea would occur to his grandfather and at the very same instant it would have come to him; one would start a sentence and the other complete it; they would tell each other their dreams and find that they issued from one and the same source.

In his view he was the most courageous of people, the most generous, the most intelligent, the wisest and the most dignified. His father was the youngest of the sons and the one who was the greatest disappointment to his father, the one most subject to his scorn. The eldest son, Abdul Kareem, had been a legend all on his own before the grandson came on the scene. It was he who travelled with camels loaded up with dates to the lands of the Kababeesh and would return driving before him herds of sheep and camels; it was he who brought goods from Egypt and the lands of the Tagali and Firteet; it was he who added land to land, houses to houses, buildings to buildings; he who built the large divan, and who brought to his father the engraved brass ewer, the sandalwood prayer beads, the ebony stick, and the prayer mat made from the skins of three leopards.

The two of them were in the diwan at the time of the afternoon siesta when Abdul Karim had come with the news of his divorce and remarriage. Speaking on behalf of his grandfather, he had said to his uncle that he was a useless man – all he was interested in was running after women. He had been less than fifteen and his uncle in his forties. They quarrelled violently, while the grand-father lay stretched out on his bed saying nothing, and the son nearly came to blows with his own uncle, who left after that and did not return. All of them broke away one by one. When the father died not one of his sons was with him. The grandson had gone far afield and arrived back when it was all over. How strange that was!

The rattle of the dry palm frond prevailed over the sound in his imagination, and he came to. He listened to the sound of the date palm frond in the wind, like the rattle of the bones of a skeleton. It had grown old now that date palm, just as he had; in its youth it had given fruit both earlier and more plentifully, of the highly prized sukkout dates. With his own hands he had planted it forty years ago and named Maryam 'the Gondeila', after its fruit. She called him Meryoud and he called her Meryoum.

The spectre of youth flickered like lightning from a distant horizon, and for a fleeting instant he sensed the flavour of dates and felt Maryam's breast pressing against his chest as they held each other in the water. Her mouth was like lightning that came and went. They would wait for her in the morning, he and Mahjoub, outside the quarter; they had with them a gown, turban and shoes, and no sooner had Maryam taken off what she was wearing and put them on than she was transformed from a girl into a boy. She used to learn as though she were remembering things she had known long ago. For three years the deception was not detected; they were up to every trick. Then nature gushed forth, with Maryam's body beginning to yield to the deepest call of life. One day the headmaster's eyes came to rest on her as she walked away from him in the school courtyard. She admitted it at once, as though she had wearied of the game. At first he was angry, then he saw the amusing aspects of the situation and off he hurried to Hajj Abdul Samad and Ali Wad Shayeb. From one day to the next Maryam was transformed, under the sway of nature's irresistible course, into another creature. She started to avert her gaze, to talk more coyly, to lower her voice when talking, and she no longer swam with them in the river or played or worked in the field. Overnight, by dint of a plot of nature and of social convention, Maryam was changed into a female and no more. And so an explosion occurred in Meheimeed's emotional life, and his attitude towards Maryam began to become clearer, more defined, and he realized that she was the natural extension to his existence, that it was she who gave him his sense of himself and of his position in the scheme of things.

From that day forth he began to back away from the role his grandfather was preparing for him; he should have fought with his own weapon but he fought with that of his grandfather and was defeated; he went away and returned only when everything was over. On that evening, when he carried Maryam's body in his arms, it was as if he were returning to the starting-point, when all possibilities were open. Did Tureifi realize, as he wept at the side of the grave, what an exorbitant price man pays that the truth about himself and about things may be made clear to him? Is he strong enough to pay the price? He, Meheimeed, had paid the price and more. Every inch of this land which he loved and then turned his back on gave witness to his having paid the price and more.

Here he rose resolutely to his feet, his limbs bracing themselves against each other, and the pain in his heart much greater than the pain in his joints, his back and his legs. He took a single step, then turned round like someone wishing to say a final word. He raised his head to the dry date palm fond. Yes, it had grown as old as he had. Its hair had fallen out as his had. He gently tapped its trunk with his stick as though comforting it and bade it farewell in an audible voice. Little wonder, for it knew his secret and his inner thoughts. After that he shuffled along the path, bearing his despair in the direction of the river.

He saw a faint light on the other bank. There was no sound except for the lisping of the tiny waves that raced after each other at his feet. Yes, there was another sound. That hum that issues from the river. Sometimes, when he was swimming, he would feel that he wouldn't care if he surrendered to that call. For a time he stayed on, throwing stones into the river as he used to do as a child and heeding the faint sound that emanated from here and there with the first glimmerings of the day: a fish leaping and diving, or a bird fluffing out its feathers in its nest.

Suddenly his whole body shuddered as though death had placed its cold hand on his shoulders. That dawn he had almost surrendered. He had been no more than seven the day his grandfather had thrown him into the river to teach him to swim. He had begun flailing about aimlessly in the water with his hands and feet, while his grandfather, some distance away, called out to him in a voice that held a certain cruelty, 'Swim. Swim.'

How to swim?

He began going under and surfacing again; the taste of the river water was the taste of death, and his grandfather's voice like that of blind destiny.

'Swim. Swim.'

He does not know what happened though he remembers the sting of the morning sun as he awoke on the bank; he remembers, too, his grandfather's laughter. He told him that he had actually swum, without assistance, not towards his grandfather ahead of him but back towards the shore, as though he had suddenly remembered something he had forgotten; he told him that he had swum like a fully grown crocodile, his chest jutting out an arm's length above the water.

After that they began to swim together every morning, each time striving more strongly towards the opposite bank. Every morning was like a last morning; it was as though death were lying in wait for him at the tip of every wave. Yet he learnt how to savour that sensation of fear, of anticipated risk, the pleasure of having scored a victory over the river when his feet touched ground in the shallow water and he stretched out flat on the edge of the bank, catching the sun's rays between his eyelids.

One morning he was almost vanquished. His grandfather had said to him that the time had come for them to swim to the whirlpool in the middle of the river. He had given a shudder when his grandfather had said that. The whirlpool, which people used to call 'the cosmic', was the meeting-place of terrible currents and was avoided by even the most accomplished swimmers. Death was for certain living in that patch of the river, like some horrible mythical animal. Yet, along with the fear, he began to feel the pleasurable sensation of danger. Then, summoning his courage, he made up his mind to sally forth on the perilous venture, even to death. His grandfather was looking at him with that glint in his eyes. His face wore the mask of death. Later, when he grew up and was better able to understand, he realized that the feeling that linked him to his grandfather at that moment just before sunrise on the river bank was one of a hatred like the flames of a fire, though it was the same sort of hatred that a man feels for himself. He didn't speak but leapt into the water; his grandfather also leapt in and the two of them swam together side by side, two or three arms' length, fifty or more years separating them: the past alongside the future, as though the two of them were a single destiny. His mind was razor-sharp, in control of every muscle in his body. He remembers the coldness of the water close into the bank; remembers the date palm trunk floating to his left; remembers a crow cawing to the east. Then he felt the water as warm, and it was as though every cell in his body were listening and seeing. He felt the noise of the whirlpool growing louder, the call growing stronger. In an instant he caught sight of Maryam's face, heard her voice calling 'Meryoud, Meryoud.' The two sounds contended with one another. Then the noise of the 'cosmic' whirlpool grew louder and louder till it prevailed over all other sounds. He doesn't remember where his grandfather was at that time; the thread binding them had snapped. He was alone, facing a destiny that was particular to him. Then he was borne off by a wave to the very centre of the chaos. It was as if a thousand bolts of lightning had struck, a thousand thunderclaps had roared. Then a silence that was not like silence reigned. He had the sensation of sitting on the throne of chaos, like a dazzling, destructive ray, as though he were a god. He wanted to kill, to destroy, to set fire to the whole universe, and to stand in the middle of the fire and to dance with the flames dancing round him. He was not only in control of the forces of his own body but of those of the river, even of all the probabilities of the future. Fear came later on. Opening his eyes like someone emerging from a nightmare, the first thing he saw was the spectre of Maryam fluttering above him. He looked and found that he had swum the whole way across the whirlpool to the other bank. He saw his grandfather going back to where he had started from. Good God, he had done the impossible, he had beaten his grandfather. He had swum the whole distance from south to north. He looked at the skin of the river crinkling and heard the fearful noise and began to tremble with fear, as ordinary mortals fear hunger, loneliness and death.

His grandfather brought the boat and took him back to the southern bank. He was rowing and talking and laughing all the way. He would tell the story to Hamad Wad Haleema and Mukhtar Wad Hasab ar-Rasoul; he would say proudly, as he did at every opportunity, 'Meheimeed is an exact replica of me, the spitting image.' But that morning the grandson went off and didn't return. He didn't have breakfast with his grandfather as they generally did after their swim; at siesta time he didn't go to read to him till he fell asleep; he didn't dine with him or sit up chatting with him as he used to do each evening, nor did he come to him first thing in the morning to drink tea with him and tell him the news of wedding feasts he'd gone off to at night with his friends Mahjoub, Taher, Abdul Hafeez and Sa'eed, of adventures, pranks and follies. By the fourth day his resentment against his grandfather for having thrown him into the face of death had lessened – and when he heard his grandfather's voice calling him his heart filled with joy and he cheered up and said yes. Perhaps everything would have gone on as it was had it not been that he had fallen in love with Maryam and that his grandfather had said no.

Suddenly he heard the sound of singing floating upon the face of the water and spreading out between the two banks, a full strong sound as though it were the sound of youth satisfied with its lot. Turning, he found that the rim of the sun had risen up resplendent, and that a boat was cleaving resolutely through the waves as though it had just emerged from the fountain-head of the rising sun, and as though the melodious singing were joining together nature's components to the two banks of the river with silken threads.

CHAPTER TWO

A s THEY were riding along on their donkeys at forenoon, on their way to the Thursday Souk, Taher Wad Rawwasi said, 'The other day you asked me a certain question and I answered you, but it's quite certain you didn't hear the reply.'

What question? And what reply? But Sa'eed the Jurist got in first. From the back of his Khandagawi donkey, nicknamed 'Second Floor', as though speaking from a dais, he said, 'From the time he returned to Wad Hamid, Meheimeed has been asking questions – you'd think he was wanting to write histories.'

Asha 'l-Baytat laughed, as did Ahmed Abu 'l-Banat.

Asha 'l-Baytat was to one side of the cavalcade, as on the left of an invading army, riding his black Kortawi donkey with a blaze on its forehead, its bridle rattling, and the long, tasselled fur covering almost touching the ground, while he, with his short legs, large turban and twirled moustache, looked like a goose sitting on a camel's hump. He said, 'I gave Meheimeed some words which should be weighed in gold and silver scales. Be careful you don't forget them when you come to write things down.'

'And where,' said Ahmed jovially, 'would someone like you get such words from, you good-for-nothing? Everything you say is a lot of rubbish.'

'Sa'eed Asha 'l-Baytat's answer was to strike the female donkey on its rump with his cane. It paid no attention and did not vary its speed, merely shaking its head proudly in the air. Asha 'l-Baytat gave it an admiring appraising look.

'Tell me, Abu 'l-Banat,' he said, 'wouldn't this donkey be the daughter of that excellent one your grandfather brought from up river?'

'The Mahasi donkey's its grandmother,' said Taher Wad Rawwasi. 'This is its granddaughter. Have you been blind or what's wrong with you, you good-for-nothing?'

'Asha 'l–Baytat's not to blame,' said Sa'eed the Jurist. 'His mind's taken up with matters of high politics. Do you imagine he's also got the time to make sure about who's the donkey's mother and who's its grandmother? By God, Taher, it's not fair of you. This is a man who's become one of the ruling class, one of the top men of the village.'

'You're right, by God,' said Taher. 'This fellow is one of the great. We're being really honoured today by having Your Excellency accompany us to the souk. You'll see after a while, friends: directly we reach the sycamore tree the guard of honour will be there to meet us, armed to the teeth and giving a military salute because of His Majesty Asha 'l–Baytat.'

'Really,' said Ahmed, 'why don't you buy yourself a Jeep like all the best people do? All this money of yours – who are you keeping it for?'

'May all Jeeps take off into the sky,' said Sa'eed the Jurist. 'Ever since Bakri's boys bought themselves their car they've ruined going into the souk for us. It's "toot toot" every other minute – they've given us a headache.'

Such talk did not anger Asha 'l–Baytat. He gave his familiar laugh and tipped his turban slightly forward, at an angle that said that Sa'eed Asha 'l–Baytat didn't give a damn about anyone.

The donkey's hooves clattered over the pebbles, making a brisk spirited tune. They were led by Sa'eed's donkey on the far left, followed by Wad Rawwasi's she-donkey that went effortlessly, like a person confident of her ability, then Sa'eed the Jurist's donkey, with Meheimeed's she-donkey in the centre, on the right flank Ahmed Abu 'l–Banats she-donkey. Some distance from them was Abdul Haffeez's donkey, going along as though on its own, hurrying then slowing down. Abdul Hafeez was silent, as he told his prayer beads; he had placed the donkey's reins on the edge of the saddle and let it go as the spirit moved it.

'There's plenty of money, thanks be to God,' said Sa'eed Asha 'l–Baytat, 'and if I wanted a Jeep there wouldn't be any difficulty about getting one. I swear, though, that a man, I don't care who he is, if he doesn't go off to the souk on a fine donkey like this and put on it a Sennari saddle and a thick hairy fur, tightening the girth and bridling it, and getting himself comfortably ensconsed, like a commander-in-chief or a police commandant, with the donkey drumming the ground with its hooves and braying "Haw

Haw" through the villages – God keep you safe, the man who doesn't do that can't be called a real man.'

'Asha Good-for-nothing seems to have the right idea,' said Taher.

'And where would he get a right idea from?' said Ahmed. 'Even if he were to buy himself a steamship he'd still be a useless good-for-nothing.'

Asha 'l-Baytat ignored all this, looked at the she-donkey and said admiringly, 'That donkey's very pleased with itself – so much so you might think it was a stag.'

The donkey stumbled and almost fell. In fright, half in earnest and half in jest, Ahmed said, 'Confound you, I knew you'd got an evil eye as hot as Hellfire – you've bewitched the animal.'

'If you want to sell it,' said Asha 'l-Baytat, 'I'll buy it from you right now.'

'What's wrong with the donkey you're riding?' said Sa'eed the Jurist. 'If your wealth is an embarrassment to you, why don't you look around for a woman to marry?'

'Asha 'l-Baytat's too old for marrying – he's better off going on the pilgrimage,' said Taher Rawwasi.

'And what will his name be then? – Hajj Asha 'l-Baytat?' said Ahmed.

'What's Asha 'l-Baytat got to do with the pilgrimage' said Taher. 'His name will then be Hajj Sa'eed.'[1]

'Sa'eed Asha 'l-Baytat gave a long laugh that hid within it many words. It was extraordinary that Abdul Hafeez too emerged from his silence and isolation and gave a short, flat laugh that made Meheimeed suddenly realize, like someone remembering some-thing, that Abdul Hafeez was with them. After that the thread of conversation was severed, for something in the reflection of the light on the surface of the water of the river made Meheimeed glance backward. He pulled at the donkey's reins and turned towards the east. From that distance it looked to him as if it was on a mound, without beginning or end, bared, like a man sleeping out in the open without a covering. The north bank was yellow, glimmering under the forenoon sun, then came the river, appear-ing and disappearing, like a mirage, like lightning. The sant and talh acacia trees clung fast to the water; adjoining them were fields of wheat, and when one's gaze came to rest on the middle, one was taken by surprise by the outburst of life there. Other fields extended to the lowest houses, after which were endless sands and desert. It all seemed to him to be suspended in a vacuum, drawing so close that it was an arm's length away, then speedily withdrawing from him like an unattainable dream.

Over there, in broad daylight, he heard their voices, and saw them with his own eyes. They called to him from the direction of the river and the desert, from east and west. He saw them coming out of the water, slipping between the branches of the trees, leaping over the tips of the date palms and the roofs of the houses, skipping about as though they were dancing on top of the domes and melting into the sun's rays.

The time was neither this nor that. Sunrise and sunset took place and repeated themselves in the blinking of an eye. He looked without fright or astonishment; then, in full command of himself, he pulled at the donkey's reins and turned his back on the sun.

CHAPTER THREE

Taher Wad Rawwasi leaned towards me without turning his face from the river, but my question remained suspended in mid-air, between river and sky. His face, the features clearly visible, shone amidst that darkness, as though light were issuing from inside him.

Suddenly he exclaimed, 'The bitch – tonight I shall get her.'

'How do you know it's a she?' I said to him.

'Even in fishes a woman's a woman and a man's a man,' he said.

In that pitch blackness I was blind, but Tahar Wad Rawwasi both heard and saw.

'The fact is she's got a blood feud on with me. Fifty years ago one of her ancestors tipped me up out of the boat. When I fell into the water she began dragging me down by my pants.'

'And what did you do?'

'I let her have the pants and came out of the water stark naked.'

His voice in that gloom was overflowing with life and merriment as though the fish in the water conversed with him in a language he understood.

'For more than three months I was after her. On one occasion she'd cut the line, on another eat the bait and bolt. The bitch, you'd think she was a genie, a species of afreet.'

I used to meet up with him at dawn on my walks, sometimes in his boat in the middle of the river, sometimes in his field, at others on the river bank, sitting and watching his line. I'd forgotten how melodious his voice was until I heard him singing that morning a song that was like a fine silken cape spread out between the two banks. Once I spotted him from afar gravely staring into the water. I called to him but he didn't answer. Some time after, in front of Sa'eed's shop, I asked him and he laughed and said, 'You saw me that day? By God, what an extraordinary thing! You might well say that as one grows old one's stricken by hallucinations. God keep you safe, for fifty years I haven't seen a thing. For fifty years I'd been fishing in the Nile and had never seen or heard a thing. That morning the bitch snapped off the hook and dived down. A little later she reared up out of the surface of the water. May God keep you safe, she'd become a human being – a young girl, stark naked. I avow my belief in God, I heard with my own ears her saying to me in a clear voice, just as you and I are talking, "Wad Rawwasi, you'd better stay away from me," and before I could find the words with which to answer her, she had dived down again with a plop into the water. As I'm your brother, Mahjoub, I just sat in stupefaction looking down into the water.'

Had Sa'eed Asha 'l-Baytat said such things to us, we would have laughed and said it was nonsense, and had Ahmed Abu 'l-Banat related it to us, we'd have said he was in his cups, but Taher Wad Rawwasi had never in his whole life told of something he hadn't actually seen or heard. As though he had only just heard the question, he now said, 'Poor Abdul Hafeez has changed from the day his daughter died. He's become another sort of person. Before he used to be wide awake and alert. Now, God knows what's come over him. Anyway, if he's found comfort in prayer, that's fine.'

'And you?'

'I? Fatima bint Jabr ad-Dar has been praying all her life – her prayers will do for both of us.'

One day I shall ask him about the story of his marriage to Fatima bint Jabr ad-Dar, one of Mahjoub's four sisters. He won't answer me now, for he's busy with the fish in the water, talking and joking with her, and has completely forgotten my presence beside him. He says to her that he caught her grandmother forty years ago, and her uncle thirty years ago, and had also caught a number of her aunts. I asked him about her parents and her brothers and sisters. Like someone waking from sleep, he said, 'Ah. Who? What?'

'What's wrong? Did you get lost in thought or what?'

'Meheimeed. I avow my belief in God, your voice came to me from very far away.'

'Her mother and father?'

'Whose mother and father?'

'The fish's.'

'Ah, the daughter of afreets, her mother is living in the middle of the river, over there. She never comes out, just now and again you'll see the movement of the waves above her.'

'And her father?'

'I think her father got married to another one up river.'

'And the brothers and sisters?'

'The brothers and sisters — some travelled up river and some down. A sister of hers capsized several boats, way up to the north.'

'And what,' I said to him in surprise, 'is keeping her here?'

'Knowledge is with God. Perhaps she's waiting for her appointed time, perhaps waiting to take her revenge on me, though I think the bitch's appointed time has come to an end this night.'

The light in the east to our right was as though awaiting a signal from someone, and the river was giving its eternal muffled scream into the ear of the bank. The bank understands nothing and the river can do nothing but speak.

At the setting of the sun the four of us were wrestling with the river in order to reach Mahjoub. Suddenly the earth swayed under our feet and in a flash the waves had flung us about to right and left. Mahjoub began sinking and coming to the surface, while the four of us — Abdul Hafeez, Hamad Wad Rayyes, Sa'eed and I — were surrounding him in a circle, trying to find a breach in the waves so as to reach him. Suddenly I spotted Taher Wad Rawwasi jumping from the shore, and it appeared to me that he was not so much swimming in the water as floating along the rays of the setting sun. He picked Mahjoub out of the water and raised him up with one hand. All at once Mahjoub came to his senses and began calling out in the darkness, cursing the river and bewailing his friend. But Taher Wad Rawwasi soon showed up from the direction of the left. We heard him laughing in the darkness. Mahjoub began cursing Wad Rawwasi as he had cursed the river. Then we all laughed at Mahjoub, at ourselves and at nothing.

Wad Rawwasi laughed on his own and said, 'Mahjoub's unbeatable on land but in the water he's absolutely hopeless.'

I smiled sadly, for the same memory came to both of us at one and the same moment: it was as though that laugh had remained locked in Was Rawwasi's breast all those years, like the remains of some fortune that had been lost, until my presence beside him that dawn had awakened it.

I talked to him so as to prompt him to remember. That same place on that same bank. Two old men watching a sunrise as though it were a sunset.

'But you, Wad Rawwasi, are unbeatable on land and in the river.'

But he was silent for so long I despaired of him. The vague sounds issuing from the river caught my attention, as though I were hearing them from a thousand miles' distance; in them were the echoes of faraway mountain wadis and cataracts. For a while I yielded to the clamour of the small waves as they untiringly raced from bank to bank. From time to time, there at the heart, where the currents meet, the river was giving vent to its old howling. Meanwhile there was a human voice to my right, which seemed to be addressing the river and the dawn that was about to break.

'O Meheimeed – life, Meheimeed, is there anything more to it than two things, friendship and love? Don't talk to me about good birth and family background, position and wealth. If a son of Adam leaves the world and has the confidence of one person, he has won. The Lord, may He be glorified, was very kind to me. Instead of one blessing He conferred on me two – He gave me the friendship of Mahjoub and the love of Fatima bint Jabr ad-Dar.'

I felt sad, for all my life I had regarded this friendship as a great honour to me. That was why I said to him gently, 'And Abdul Hafeez, and Sa'eed, and . . .?'

'Abdul Hafeez is a brother to me,' he said, 'so is Sa'eed, but the human being, the brother, the friend, the man who's worth a thousand men – we're talking about the heart, deep, deep inside. It's not about Taher Wad Rawwasi – what it's really about is Taher the son of Bilal, the son of Hawwa, the slave.

He said this with simplicity, without any bitterness, then added, 'You were away, you were travelling. You'd be away for a year and come and stay with us for a month or two – from early on, from your schooldays and, later, when you were working in the government. The person who's with you isn't like the person who's far away, no matter what!'

Then he said, 'The woman who says she's given birth to some-one like Mahjoub Wad Jabr ad-Dar is a liar.'

He fell silent in a natural manner, as though wanting to entrust this sentence to the custody of the dawn's conscience, wanting to make sure that the river too had heard and understood.

He then occupied himself with the line and hook, pulling it in, then letting it go. Then he sent it out and paid no attention to it, as though the fish was no longer of any interest to him. He laughed and turned towards me and I saw his dark face was like a piece of coal, shining that dawn as though it radiated with lights of faraway stars. He laughed some more and said, 'Let's leave the subject of Abdul Hafeez. You just asked me about Abdul Hafeez, but I know the thing you really want to hear about. Why is it that all these years you haven't asked me? I wouldn't have told you though. Never in my life have I sat with a soul and indulged in chit-chat. It's not that the story isn't known. Part of it people know and part they don't know, and the part they don't know isn't worth telling now. They do say though, that old age loosens the tongue, and what's left to life but conversation? I'll tell you something else – all this time I was hiding the story in my heart, wanting to tell it to someone. Not to Mahjoub – Mahjoub knows it and more. No, to someone else, someone with compassion and understanding who knows bits of it and is unfamiliar with other bits. Someone like you, Meheimeed. There is something about you which encourages one to say things to you that one wouldn't ordinarily say to a soul.'

Gusts of wind blew in from the east, small and warm, causing a ripple in the water, a rustle among the branches of the trees, which quickly died down.

'The fact is,' said Was Rawwasi, 'this is an age of talk – broadcasts, cinemas, newspapers, schools, unions and what have you. The other day I heard the radio booming out about workers, peasants, socialism, social justice, increased production, protection of the revolution's gains, opportunism and reactionaries – brothers, what sort of catastrophe has befallen us? This useless radio barking away all day long, won't its voice ever let up? I said to Hajj Sa'eed, "Tell me, Hajj, these workers and peasants, where are they from". He said to me, "You fool, the workers and peasants are none other than us." "Good Heavens, are we now called workers and peasants?" "Yes," he said to me. "All right, and what does increased production mean?" He said to me, "Isn't production this god-forsaken work that we do? – so increased production means doing even more of it." Afterwards Hajj Sa'eed laughed and said to me, "Why don't you go and ask Tureifi Wad Bakri to explain all those words to you. Surely you see him every day gathering up the likes of Sa'eed Asha 'l-Baytat and giving them long lectures?" '

He was silent for a while, then said, 'Perhaps what's happened is all for the good. Who knows? As this sort of chat we're having gets acted out on the radio, is made into films and printed in books, why don't you get down to work and record it, Meheimeed? Who knows, it might be a lesson to those who would take heed.'

And so Taher Wad Rawwasi proceeded to weave, from the threads of the dawn advancing upon us, the fabric of his life story. His voice rose and fell, with the wind sometimes blowing strongly and drowning his words. At others it seemed to me that all the elements of nature had grown quiet and were listening closely to what he was saying.

His talking diverted my attention from watching the dawn break, and I did not wake up to the fact until the light of sunrise had touched the tips of the date palms and the trees and had spread onto the water's surface.

'Thanks be to God,' said Wad Rawwasi. 'Thanks be to God.'

Then he said, 'My friend, tonight we've chatted a lot, but because of the talk we've failed to catch ourselves a good lunch. This bitch of a fish saw how preoccupied we were talking and has eaten the bait and bolted.'

Directing his words at the fish's imaginary mother out in the middle of the Nile, he said, 'You woman over there, tell your daughter that she'd better keep away from me. The next time, whether she flies off or sits tight, she won't get away from me.'

After that he guffawed with laughter and jumped to his feet.

'Brother,' he said, 'up you get and let's get going. Bint Jabr ad-Dar will have prepared morning tea.'

So we made our way up towards the houses, I leaning on my stick, the ebony one, and he walking in front of me with strong, energetic strides. He began to sing some poetry that I had heard from him in another time and at another place.

CHAPTER FOUR

٤

HIS NAME was Hasan but people called him Bilal[2] because, when giving the call to prayer, his voice was beautiful and he was incapable of pronouncing certain Arabic sounds correctly.

They said it was Sheikh Nasrullah Wad Habib who gave him the name when he heard his voice. He taught him the call to prayer and made him a muezzin. He used to say to him, 'Blessed are those who attend the dawn prayer in the mosque in answer to your voice, Bilal. By God, your voice is not of this world but has come down from heaven.'

Sometimes they would call him, 'Halla Halla, son of no-god-but-God.' As for the 'Halla Halla', this was because it was the only expression uttered by him when addressed, and as for 'no-god-but-God', this was because, when asked about his father, he would answer, 'I'm the son of no-god-but-God.'

Those who have seen him relate that he had a beautiful face and was of handsome appearance with well-proportioned limbs; neither particularly tall nor short, with a complexion that glowed like the colour of musk. His beauty was such that one could not gaze at him for any length of time. A very serene person with a regal expression, he had noble features and demeanour, as though descended from a line of ancient kings. When he rose, it was as if an unseen retinue rose with him, and when he sat down he would do so squatting on his heels and would remain absolutely still as though melting into his surroundings. They related that he used to walk leaning forward towards the ground, that he did not speak much and that, standing or sitting, he would go on looking down at the ground, his tongue untiringly uttering the names of God and calling down blessings on His Prophet. Sheikh Nasrulla Wad Habib, despite his elevated position, would stand up when he entered, would show him affection and would insist that he sit beside him, and would see him out when he left. They said that such respect from that venerable Sheikh would make Bilal weep and he would say to him, 'My lord, this is not permissible from the likes of you to the likes of me. I am your slave and you are my master by the will of God.'

'O Bilal,' the Sheikh would say to him, 'you are the slave of God just as I am the slave of God. We are brothers in the sight of God. You and I are like specks of dust in the kingdom of God, may He be glorified. And on the day when a father will not be compensated for by his son,[3] it is possible that your scale will outweigh mine in the balances of the Truth, may His Majesty be exalted. My scale outweighs yours in the balances of the people of the world, but your scale, O Bilal, will outweigh mine in the Balance of Justice. I, Bilal, run like a thirsty camel in order to attain a drop from the Cup of the Presence, while you, Bilal, have drunk to the full. You have heard and you have seen; you have crossed and you have passed over; and when the voice called you, you said yes. You said yes. You said yes.'

The Sheikh would weep until his beard was wet, and Bilal would say to him, weeping, 'No, master. No, master. You are my Sheikh and my Axis,[4] my lord and my master. I am your slave and your bondman in the sight of God.'

Those who were contemporaries of his relate that when he was giving the call to the dawn prayer, you would have the sensation that the voice was not reaching you from the mosque's minaret but was issuing forth from your own heart. It was, as they recount, an extraordinary thing when Bilal Halla Halla would give the call and Sheikh Nasrullah Wad Habib would lead the people in prayer. Each morning the mosque would be filled with the faithful. Each morning prayers would be attended by a mass of worshippers, strangers whom people had not previously seen. The doors of heaven were, at that period of time, opened, as they said, and when the two of them died the shadows of mercy were rolled up and the doors of sovereignty were locked, right up to this very day.

Taher Wad Rawwasi says that the sole name he inherited from his father was a nickname by which no one but Al-Kashif Rahmat-allah called him. Wad Rahmatallah used to say that Bilal was a boatman,[5] and they would ask him what sort of boatman and he would reply, 'Bilal is the boatman of the boats of Omnipotence.' He swears that he has seen him several times between night and dawn standing alone in a boat taking strange-looking people across to the other bank. Taher says that when his father died he took all his names with him, as though he were in actuality a unique soul, not one of our souls of this time nor yet of this earth.

They said that he lived on for only one year after the death of Sheikh Nasrullah Wad Habib and that he died at the same hour of the same day in the month of Rajab. After the death of his Sheikh, he had given up making the call to prayer and going to the mosque and had disappeared from sight. Then, one day, the people had awoken to his voice calling out from the minaret of the mosque, a voice that those who heard it described as being like that of a conglomeration of voices coming from diverse places and bygone ages, and that Wad Hamid had trembled at the vastness of the voice and had begun to extend and grow bigger, to grow higher and wider, as though it were some other city in some other time. Every one of them rose from his bed, made his ablutions and hurried off to the source of the voice, as if the call that dawn were meant for him alone. When they were standing ready for prayers, they saw Bilal wearing a shroud. The mosque was crammed with a great concourse of people, both inhabitants from the village and people from outside. It was a strange sight. As he used to do in the days of Wad Habib, he started prayers with the words 'God is great,' then took his place to lead them in prayer. He did not stand in front of them as the Sheikh used to do but took his place among them in the centre of the first row, dressed as he was. He recited the Chapter of the Forenoon in a joyful voice, the verses coming out as radiant as clusters of grapes. After prayers, he turned to them with a happy, glowing face and said farewell to them, asking of them that they should not carry him on a bier but on their shoulders and that they should bury him alongside his Sheikh, Nasrullah Wad Habib, while leaving between the Sheikh and him such space as the dictates of respect and reverence demanded. After that he stretched out on the ground by the prayer niche, uttered the avowal of faith and asked forgiveness of God, while the people looked on in awe and astonishment; then he raised his hand as though greeting someone and yielded up his soul to its Maker. They bore him off, from that place in the mosque, to the cemetery, and they said that so many people walked in his funeral procession it was as though the earth had opened up and spilt them out. They buried him, as they relate, at sunrise and they were led in prayer by a man of awe-inspiring appearance, whose face no one had ever seen before, though most of them said that he looked like Sheikh Nasrullah Wad Habib. They narrated that there was not a man that witnessed the death of Bilal who did not wish his own soul might be snatched away at that very instant, for he had made the taste of death in their mouths to be as that of honey.

Taher Wad Rawwasi said that his father had grown up as a slave without a master, one left to his own devices, all the other slaves – with the exception of Bilal – possessing masters. It is said that he was perhaps one of the offspring of the slaves that had belonged to the king called Bandarshah, who had ruled that province in olden times. About this Bandarshah there are conflicting versions. Some storytellers in Wad Hamid claim that he was one of the Christian kings of Nubia, whose authority had spread southwards to the lands of the Manaseer and northwards to the frontiers of Egypt, and that the capital of the kingdom was where Wad Hamid lies today. He was a mighty and invincible king who mobilized armies, built warships that sailed on the Nile, constructed citadels and fortresses, put up churches, and levied taxes on trading caravans; then, when the Arab armies came in, this Bandarshah opposed them. However, they utterly defeated him, rending his forces to pieces, taking his women captive and plundering his belongings and slaves. It is said that some of Bandarshah's slaves embraced Islam, while others were scattered throughout the country, northwards and southwards.

In another version, it is related that this king was not a Christian, but a pagan king who had raided that province with a large army of black troops from the upper reaches of the Nile, and that he had set up, in the area of Wad Hamid and its neighbourhood, a strong black kingdom that continued to hold supreme sway till it was destroyed by Abdullah Jammaa during the time of the ascendency of the kingdom of Sennar. They said that his name was not Bandarshah but Bengeh or Jangeh and that what remained of his offspring and troops were enslaved every single one of them after having been free men.

Some historians think it likely that Bandarshah was an Abyssinian prince called Menderse who, because of the struggles for the kingdom in the days of King Ras Tefari the Great, fled with his women and children and a number of his soldiers and slaves; that they crossed the Nile at al-Matamma, then traversed the Bayouda desert till they arrived at the bend of the river where Wad Hamid now lies, and that they found a high hill overlooking a wide, fertile plain protected by desert lying beyond it, eastwards and westwards, with rocky hills to the south and the river to the north. There they settled and built a town they named Deboras, which is to say 'the hill' in their tongue, as legends relate. They said that this Prince Menderse found there some stone temples from past ages, which he demolished, building from the stones a lofty palace on top of the hill, a masterpiece of beautiful architecture and an impregnable fortress that continued to withstand the ravages of time. They mentioned that this prince's power was so great that he began raiding northwards and southwards in the later Christian era and that he imposed the Jizya[6] on the princes of the neighbouring states, and that then, at the height of his power, he had gathered together a large army with which he had crossed the Bayouda desert in a straight line from west to east, had crossed the Nile at Berber, and had then taken his army along the river to Atbara. He had continued on his way towards the land of Abyssinia having the intention to wrest the kingdom from the ruling Negus. The Negus's armies had met up with him on the frontiers and they had fought together for many days. Then, launching a powerful attack against him, they had killed him and smashed his army, scattering it to the winds. It is further mentioned that those who were left behind were absorbed into the rest of the races that made up the inhabitants, and it is said that among the remnants of them is a small tribe in Wad Hamid called 'the sons of the son of the Habashi', who are famous for the good looks of their men and the beauty of their women.

A further version says that Bandarshah was neither this nor that but was a man of fair complexion who had arrived in Wad Hamid – no one knows from where – at the time of the raids and battles in the final days of the kings of Sennar. Wad Hamid was there then, being well-populated and known by the same name as it goes by today. He had settled in it and began to operate in the slave trade, making a vast fortune. It is said that he employed his slaves in the cultivation of tobacco, something that the village did not know before his time, or after his time. He used to bring slaves and elephants' tusks from the Upper Nile and would take them in great camel caravans to Berber, Suakim and Egypt. From this he made himself untold wealth. Supporters of this version assert that this is the Bandarshah who built the palace on top of the hill, bringing to it marble columns and ceramic tiles and making its roof of beech wood and teak; he also provided it with a gate from haraz wood that measured two cubits in breadth. They related that in this palace there were about fifty rooms opening out on to a vast courtyard in the centre, and that it had stables for horses, stockades for camels and enclosures for cattle and sheep, and that the house was provided with constant running water summer and winter. This was accomplished by having slaves raise the water from an enormous well into a larger water tower built at a great height and from which the water would run down in channels to all parts of the palace. They have likewise described how a person entering would find at the palace gate tall, strong, black guards, girded with swords, who would be standing watch night and day. One would cross the vast courtyard, then mount some steps to find further guards standing on both sides of a thick door, through which one would enter and find oneself in a great rectangular hall. On the side facing the door was a raised dais on which stood a large throne of black wood with ivory armrests, ending in an ivory carving of a crouching lion. They said that the hall was lit by lanterns hanging from the ceiling and that it was redolent with the aroma of incense rising from burners placed in wall recesses. They told that this Bandarshah's greatest pleasure was to sit on that throne of a night, after eating his fill and drinking till he was drunk, then order his slaves to be herded in, shackled in irons. He would order his executioners to flog them with thick whips made of hippopotamus hide until the blood flowed from their backs and they fainted, when he would order them to be dragged out. Then he would clap his hands and naked slave-girls would enter the hall, dancing and singing and beating on drums or playing the tambourines till he would grow sleepy. No sooner did he yawn than the hall would empty and his slaves would carry him out to his bedroom. They said that Bandarshah carried on like this for some time, inflicting the direst punishments on his slaves, not for any sins they had committed but for his own pleasure and amusement. This went on till the night they rebelled as one man and fell upon him and killed him, then they hacked him to pieces and threw them into the palace well. After that they set fire to the palace and its contents and made their escape under cover of night. They left behind them no one but young children and old men and women. They said that the palace remained on for a long time, after the slaves had burnt it down, in the state in which it was till it was seen by the Emir Yunis Wad Dukeim, who ruled that district during the days of the Mahdi. When he saw it he stopped, amazed by its appearance. Asking the local people about who had built it, they gave him conflicting reports. He stared at the lofty building for some time, repeating, 'God is Omnipotent. God is Omnipotent!' Then he said, 'This building was not built by man – this is the work of devils,' and he ordered his troops to destroy what remained of it, and they razed it to the ground. Today nothing remains of it but fragments of stone and shards buried in high mounds of earth heaped up above where the citadel used to be.

As for Ibrahim Was Taha, who is a reliable chronicler of Wad Hamid's history, he asserts that Bilal was not one of the slaves of a Christian king, nor of an Abbysinian prince, nor yet of a pagan king, nor anything of the sort. Rather was his master a person known by everyone, being neither of unknown origin nor of questionable descent, but was Isa Wad Dau al-Beit. It is a fact that Dau al-Beit, Isa's father, was a man of the Sherifs[7] who had come to Wad Hamid from the Hejaz and settled there. He had married the original Fatima bin Jabr ad-Dar from the Hawamida tribe, people of noble stock and lords of Wad Hamid after whom the village was named – not to be confused with the other Wad Hamid which is to be found in the south near the town of Shendi. Ibrahim Wad Taha says that Bandarshah was a nickname by which Isa Wad Dau al-Beit was known in his youth, it being in the nature of a joke among the young boys, and was conferred on him by his cousin on his mother's side, Hamid Wad Abdul Khalek Wad Hamad, known as Wad Haleema.

Ibrahim Wad Taha says that Jabr ad-Dar, the grandson of Hamid the Great, who was the originator of the name, had one son, Rajab, who became known by the nickname of Allah Leena because of his cowardice, and four daughters, every one of whom was the equal of a hundred men: Haleema, Maryam, Maymouna and Fatima. As for Haleema, she married Abdul Khalek Wad Hamad; Maryam married Sheikh Mahmoud Wad Ahmed Wad Hamid, Jabr ad-Dar's cousin, who was the leader of the village in his time; Maymouna married Hasab ar-Rasoul Wad Mukhtar, the son of Hasab ar-Rasoul, who was nicknamed the Gallant, a man of great chivalry and hospitality, while Fatima, the youngest and most outstanding of them, married Dau al-Beit by whom she had one son, Isa Wad Dau Al-Beit, whose father died while he was in his mother's womb, leaving him great wealth. His mother used to spoil him when he was small and would dress him up in expensive and colourful clothes that were unknown to the villagers. For this reason the boys would tease him and call him by a strange name which did not stick to him for very long and which, with the passing of the day, was forgotten. It was this Fatima who was the originator of the 'Sons of Dau', a subdivision of the Hawamida tribe.

Ibrahim Wad Taha relates that Isa Wad Dau al-Beit married the daughter of his maternal uncle, Rajab, by whom he had eleven sons. She gave him a son every two years as regular as clockwork and she continued to give birth even after her sons became fathers. It would sometimes happen that she would be confined in childbed while alongside her would be the wife of a son of hers also so confined. She went on like this till she died, not yet having attained the age of forty.

Ibrahim Wad Taha affirms that Bilal was the twelfth of Isa Wad Dau al-Beit's sons, born of a beautiful and intelligent black slave-girl whom he had loved greatly. He did not, however, recognize him as his legal son, and when the father died his brothers, though ashamed to make a slave of him, were too proud to treat him as a free man and to share with him his father's inheritance. Thus Bilal grew up neither free and called the son of So-and-so, not yet a slave and called the slave of So-and-so. He was a man apart: of pleasing appearance and disposition, chaste and godly, and with a distinguished and noble character. It was wondrous that he should have grown up as though he had all of a sudden descended from the sky, or as though he had sprouted forth from the earth, or emerged from the Nile, a person wholly formed and shaped. For not a soul in the village remembers him as a child, nor does anyone know who brought him up, not is there anyone who will say to you 'I saw Bilal' or 'I heard Bilal', until suddenly he had made his appearance as a grown-up young man who used to be constantly in the company and at the service of Sheikh Nasrullah Wad Habib. Suddenly the villagers had woken up to this glorious person whose beauty stole one's heart, whose voice would cause rock to crumble, iron to turn soft. When he called out at dawn in his accented voice, 'I bear witness that there is no god but God, and I bear witness that Mohammed is the Messenger of God', you would feel that the whole of Wad Hamid, its inhabitants and its animals, its trees and its stones, its sand and its mud, from its lowest parts to its highest, from its land to its water, had quaked and quivered and been stricken with a trembling. His call was not a call to prayer but rather a call of life since the time of Adam and the call of death since Gabriel and Israfeel[8] and Mika'eel[9] and Azreal[10]. Every day he would give the call to the five prayers, not missing a single day, until Sheikh Nasrullah Wad Habib died, when he stopped and disappeared from sight, until his memorable call to prayer on the day of his death. He would always close the night and dawn calls to prayer with the words, 'Hurry, O people. O people, the boat has set sail. The sea is deep. The people of God have set out on the road. This is the time of the Owner of Time, the Sultan of the Age. This is the time of Nasrullah Wad Habib. This is the time of Nasrullah Wad Habib.'

They said that he first became a disciple of Sheikh Nasrullah Wad Habib when he was a young man between the ages of fifteen and twenty. Perhaps he used to roam afar into the desert making acts of devotion and worship to God – nobody knows – because he was not to be seen in the village, as though he didn't exist. One day when the people were gathered in a circle round Sheikh Nasrullah Wad Habib after the dawn prayer – it was his custom, after finishing the dawn prayer and the night prayer, to stay on for a period of an hour or so to teach people and answer their questions – he suddenly fell silent for a while, a change coming over his face, and then shouted at the top of his voice, 'Come to us, Bilal. Come to us, Bilal.'

The people did not understand what the Sheikh meant.

'Who are you calling to, O Sheikh?' they said to him.

'Bilal the blessed,' he answered them in a different tone. 'Bilal the blessed, Bilal the blessed,' repeating it three times in this manner.

They still did not understand, relapsing into silence as they thought for a while. Suddenly, as though inspiration had descended upon him, one of them said, 'The Sheikh means Hasan.'

When they asked the speaker to identify which Hasan he meant, he was at a loss as to how to describe him. Then, as though the truth had manifested itself to them all at once, they called out together, 'Hasan, Halla Halla – the slave.'

It was then that Sheikh Nasrullah Wad Habib, being in a trance-like state, addressed them, 'Bilal is not anyone's slave. Bilal is the slave of God. Were you but to know about it as I do, your hearts would be split open in awe and you would be seized by terror and confusion. He has seen and he has heard and he has attained such heights of holiness unattainable to all but a chosen few. By God, were Bilal to ask something of God, He would fulfil it for him, and were he to request of the Truth, glorified be He, to make the earth swallow you up, He would do so.'

The Sheikh said this in a voice that struck his listeners with terror, then he began calling out anew.

'Come to us, Bilal. Come to us, Bilal.'

They swore that no sooner had Sheikh Nasrullah Wad Habib finished calling them they heard a voice crying out at the door of the mosque, 'Here I am. At your service.'

He entered, the dust of far journeying upon him, round his neck a long string of prayer beads made of the kernels of the laloub tree, and in his hand a leather water-bottle. He knelt at the Sheikh's feet, kissing them as he repeated, 'At your service. At your service.' The Sheikh raised him to his feet, embraced and kissed him on his cheeks and his forehead. The Sheikh's eyes streaming with tears, he said to him, 'Why, brother, do you go so far away from me? Haven't you and I suffered enough? Treat yourself gently, my dear one, for you have come to occupy a rank that but few of the humble devout have attained. I run and scarcely keep up with your dust.'

They said that Bilal wept so much that he almost departed this life, as he repeated, 'Master, do not say such things. You are the Axis. You are the master of the time and I am your servant and your slave.'

They said that the Sheikh wanted to treat him like a brother, but he absolutely refused and insisted that he would accept no relationship to the Sheikh except that of a slave to his master. The Sheikh gave in, despite his heart's refusal, and Bilan was at Sheikh Nasrullah Wad Habib's service night and day, filling for him his ewer for making ablutions and serving his food. When the Sheikh went walking in the heat of the day he would hold above his head a large green umbrella, and if the Sheikh happened to go for a ride – which he seldom did – he would accompany him on foot, holding the reins of his mount. He would refuse to sit with the Sheikh, content to stand, or to crouch at the other's feet like a faithful dog. When Sheikh Nasrullah Wad Habib saw him acting like this he would say to him, 'O Bilal. O Bilal. Why do you want to rebuke us by humiliating yourself?'·

They said that Sheikh Nasrullah Wad Habib was indisputably the Axis of his time. People used to come to him from the corners of the earth in search of his learning and to gain grace from being in his company; they would come to him in camel caravans from the lands of Morocco, Tunisia, Egypt and Syria, from the countries of the Hausa and the Fulani, bringing him precious gifts, none of which he took into his own house, but would distribute to the people at his gatherings. When the Imam Mohammed Ahmed the Mahdi started on his religious crusade, he wrote to the Sheikh calling upon him to recognize him as Imam and be one of his followers. Sheikh Nasrullah Wad Habib wrote back saying, 'We would inform you that we do not obey the orders of anyone but the one and only King. If you are a rightly guided one, then God the Omnipotent, the Most High, will increase you in guidance, for He is the Owner of the Glory and chooses those He favours from among His servants, so proceed in accordance with God's Book and the sunna[11] of the Prophet and you will not go astray, by the name of the most Holy Ruler, the Merciful, the Compassionate who guides those whom He wishes and leads astray those whom He wishes, He gives sway to those He wishes and divests of kingship those whom He wishes.' And they related that he did not concern himself with the Mahdi, neither supporting nor rejecting him, letting his companions do as they pleased and not dissuading any of them who wished to join up with the originator of that cause, though only a small band of them went. When the Khalifa Abdulla at-Ta-ayshi succeeded the Mahdi, he sent word to Sheikh Nasrullah Wad Habib to come to him in Omdurman. The Sheikh answered him in rough terms and the Khalifa was angered and sought to send some of his soldiers to arrest him and bring him by force. But the Khalifa was thwarted and did not do any of the things he had intended. And they said that Sheikh Nasrullah Wad Habib used to say, having in mind the Khalifa Abdulla at-Ta-ayshi, 'By God, by God other than whom there is no god, when Moslem princes are filled with vanity and are seduced by the transient world, and their dominant positions and their many followers delight them, and they become drunk with the cup of power, and it appears to them that they are strong, having become immortal in their prison cells, God smites them with the sceptre of His might and breaks their backs with the sword of His vengeance, and He makes the sword of the infidels to be given mastery over them and establishes their enemies against them, and He brings out from their hidden lairs those who will plot their downfall and will fight against them till conqueror and conquered, seeker and sought, are annihilated and are transformed into the hollow stumps of date palms or are become as particles of dust scattered by the wind on a day of desolation, as God did with the people of Aad and Thamud,[12] so make haste, make haste.'

They said that there was in Wad Hamid a woman of stunning beauty called Hawwa bint al-Oreibi; she had come down from the lands of the Kababeesh with her parents in the years of drought and famine. Her parents having died and being left on her own, she made her living by doing people's hair, and spinning and working in the houses of the well-to-do in the village. They described her face as being like the break of day, her hair black as night and hanging down her back to her buttocks, and that she was tall and well-proportioned, with long eyelashes and smooth of cheek, and it was as if she had a comb of honey in her mouth. She was in addition exceedingly intelligent and bold with a degree of coquettishness and obscenity in her speech. Many wanted her, among them certain wealthy villagers, but she was unassailable. She kept her honour, accepting no pursuer, be it lawfully or in sin.

They said that the heart of this Hawwa became attached to no one but Bilal and that she would accost him when he was at his prayers and devotions and he would not reply or respond to her. At first people thought she was merely amusing herself with him, then they became convinced that she had, strange to say, fallen in love with him in such a way that she was almost beside herself. When she was at her wits' end, she went to Sheikh Nasrullah Wad Habib and told him of her suffering, humbling herself and beseeching him, at which he urged Bilal to marry her. Bilal said to him, 'O master, I would sacrifice my life for you, but there is no secret about the circumstances of your humble servant that is hidden from you. I am walking in the paths of the people of the Presence and yet you order me to do the actions of the people of this world.'

The Sheikh said to him, 'O Bilal, to walk in the paths of union is like ascending rugged mountain tracks. The wish of the Truth is obscure, O Bilal; the love of certain servants is from the love of God, and this poor woman loves you in a way that I do not find is of the kind of love of this world's people, and it may be that the Truth has sent her for you for some purpose of His. Perhaps He, glorified be His wish, wants you to test the extent of your own love in the balance of this poor woman's love for you. Either you surrender and your journey is interrupted, or your thirst for the cup of Eternal Love is increased when He, be He glorified and exalted, will have accomplished His wish by subjecting you to His ultimate will.'

Bilal complied with his Sheikh's order and married Hawwa.

They said that he came together with her for only one night. After that he asked permission of his Sheikh to release him from his obligation, to which the Sheikh consented. She conceived from him that night of a son who was named Taher and who became generally known by the name of Taher Wad Rawwasi. After Bilal had released her from the ties of marriage, she refused to be with another man and devoted herself to bringing up her son, doing so with that devotion known only to single-minded Sufis. It is said that when she passed away, being over seventy years old, her beauty was in no way diminished – time had changed her not at all, it being as though she had lived impervious to its vicissitudes.

Taher Wad Rawwasi says, 'I have not seen love like that of this mother; I have not seen tenderness like hers. She filled my heart with love until I became like an inexhaustible spring. On the Day of Reckoning, when mankind stands before the Glorious, the Magnificent, bearing their prayers and their almsgiving, their pilgrimage and their fastings, their night vigils in prayer and their worship, I shall say "O Owner of Majesty and Might, Your wretched servant, Taher Wad Bilal, the son of Hawwa bint al-Oreibi, stand before You empty-handed, devoid of merit, having nothing to place in the scales of Your justice but love." '

CHAPTER FIVE

S A'EED ASHA 'L–BAYTAT gave the call to prayer that dawn with a voice like a magnet, to which clung the dust of unfulfilled dreams, while squalls of Amsheer echoed Maryam's call, 'Meryoud. Meryoud. You are nobody. You are nothing, Meryoud.'

She met me at the door. I saw her appearing and disappearing until the people said, 'And not those that are astray. Amen.'[13] The whole universe was fragrant with the perfume that had pursued me all those years, reminding me of Maryam counting up on her fingers and saying, 'Ahmed, Mohammed, Mahmoud, Hamid, Hamad, Hamdan . . .'[14]

'The sons are more than the names available, Maryoum.'[15]

'We'll make them up to ten with girls,' she said, laughing.

We buried her at sunset as though we were planting a date palm or depositing in the earth some precious secret which would, in some form or other, bear fruit in the future. Mahjoub kissed her cheek, and I kissed her forehead, while Tureifi almost perished from weeping. Gently the six of us carried her and placed her on the side of the grave. I hear that voice the like of which there is no other, coming to me from afar like a magic flute in a mantle of moonlights on summer nights, and the flash of rays of light on the damp fronds of date palms and the blaze of blossom in orchards of oranges. Dragging my turban from my head, she says, 'We'll live in the city. Do you hear? Water from the tap and light by electricity, and travel by train. Got it? Cars and all the latest inventions. Hospitals and schools and this and that. In the city. Got it? God curse Wad Hamid. It's just a heap of ashes. It gives you nothing but disease, death and headaches. All our children will become effendis. Got it? No more farming. By the life of my brother Mahjoub, let's have no more farming, ever.'

I felt her so light in my arms as I lowered her into the grave. Her breast was pressing against my chest as we held each other in the water, diving and surfacing. She lowered her gaze and I lowered mine, and after that she didn't go to school any more. The secret was out. I would annoy her with my laugh and would ask her about what our children would be and she would give it serious thought and say, counting off on her fingers, 'Ahmed will be a governor.'

'A governor of what?'

'A governor of anything.'

'Bravo! And Mohammed?'

'Mohammed will be a lawyer.'

'Excellent, but wouldn't it be better for him to be a judge?'

'A lawyer, so he can defend those who have been wrongly accused. They say judges go to hell.'

'Fine. And Mahmoud?'

'Mahmoud – Mahmoud – Mahmoud will be a doctor.'

'You don't say! And Hamid?'

'Hamid will also be a doctor.'

'My! My! You've become Mother of Doctors. And the fifth – what's his name? – what will he be?'

'Hamad. Hamad will be an engineer.'

'An engineer? God is great. And the sixth?'

'Hamdan will be a master.'

'A station master?'

'A headmaster.'

'Like that of Wad Hamid's school?'

'Let's hope Wad Hamid will sink into the ground. No, of a large school built of stone and red brick and set among gardens.'

'And the rest of the illustrious ten?'

'Whether the rest turn out to be boys or girls, they'll all be teachers and doctors.'

'The girls too?'

'Why not?'

'Right – and how are you going to produce all this nation? By the time the tenth one arrives you'll be fifty.'

'Not at all – twenty at most if we start next year.'

'We're getting married next year?'

'Why not?'

I'd laugh and roll about in the sand from laughing so much, for I wasn't yet thirteen and Maryam was less than ten. She'd hit me on the chest and back with both fists and pull at my turban and gown, getting really worked up.

I'd sit and say to her with mock seriousness, while I counted off on the fingers of her hand, 'Listen here, you silly girl. Our children will come out as follows: Ahmed a farmer. Mohammed a farmer. Hamad will become head of the tramps. Hamid will become a chanter, glorifying the Prophet like Hajj al-Mahi of old and Mohammed Wad Sa'eed today in al-Affad.'

'The Prophet, may the blessings and peace of God be upon him,'[16] Maryam corrected me angrily. Then she added her wide, honey-coloured eyes sparking with rage, 'Mohammed comes before Mahmoud.'

'Whether he comes before or after it's all one – all of them will be farmers.'

'And what about Hamdan?' Maryam would say, like an eagle about to swoop down.

I'd be silent for a while, scarcely able to hold back my laughter, while Maryam's chest would rise and fall in rage.

'I've got a big position in mind of Hamdan. Hamdan, my pretty lady, will be the chief – the chief of the robbers of the northern province.'

She would claw with her fingernails at my face and hit me with her small fists, bite me and kick me, while I laughed and rolled about in the sand as she screamed, 'Never. Never. Never.'

While so engaged, Mahjoub would come along and I'd tell him the story.

'Why put off getting married till next year?' he would say. 'Right away, tomorrow, we'll make out the contract. Maryam is ripe for marriage and we can't make her wait a further year.'

We'd go on teasing her like that till she'd run away from us in tears.

We were, though, the two persons most dear to her: I being the pivot of her dreams of the future in the city, and Mahjoub being her sole brother amidst four girls, of whom Maryam was the youngest. I looked at him in the middle of the crowd that evening, enveloped by the rays of the setting sun, fierce and angry, as though death were an adversary sent against him by the government. In a husky voice he gave orders and the people submitted themselves to his authority. That evening he was a leader with absolute power, as he would never be again, vital and alert, like an animal of prey ready to spring at any moment, but the power of death could not be conquered. As for myself, I was sad in another way. I was seeing her swimming on a wave, approaching and receding, while the world was smiling with the face of a child. Her honey-coloured eyes were crowding the face, her noble eyebrows joined up above them, while her mouth was like lightning that comes and goes. Tureifi was crying till he almost perished, while I had in my heart a sensation of calamity that was like exaltation. They continued digging the grave and I saw Maryam as a child of less than four, reading the Qur'an with us in the Koranic school of Sheikh Saad. She did this out of sheer determination, nothing standing in the way of her strong desire to solve the riddle of the characters. She would come and we would chase her away, but she wouldn't be chased off, and we would be forced, Mahjoub and I, to teach her — it was as though we had released a genie from a bottle. She began to read, to learn by heart and to understand until she caught up with us and almost outstripped us. She would contend with us, verse by verse and chapter by chapter, till we got fed up with her competing with us. When we joined the school we were happy to be learning things she did not understand, and we would come back and read to her about history, geography, and arithmetic, which would annoy her. So she began to ingratiate herself with us and to beseech us to take her with us.

'School's for boys,' we said to her. 'There are no girls at school.'

As though she had given the matter due consideration, she said, 'Perhaps if they saw me they'd accept me.'

'And what's so extraordinary about you,' I said, laughing, 'that if they saw you they'd accept you?'

'Do you think yourself a beauty?' added Mahjoub. 'You're ugly and thin as a grasshopper.'

She paid no attention to our teasing.

'Perhaps if they saw me reading and writing,' she said seriously. 'Isn't it all a matter of reading and writing? What's the difference between boys and girls?'

That's how the government system is,' said Mahjoub. 'A boys' school means a school for boys. Do you want the government to make a special system for you?'

'Why not?' she said.

We laughed because that was Maryam's way: to think that everything was possible. Suddenly, having turned the matter over in her sharp mind and arrived at a solution, she said, with her beautiful and intelligent eyes looking out above our heads to the distance.

'Right – seeing that the government accepts only boys, I'll become a boy.'

We suppressed our astonishment and sought to find out from her what she had in mind.

'That's to say I'll go along with you to school as though I'm a boy.'

'*You* become a boy?' Mahjoub asked her scornfully.

And then I asked her with even more scorn. '*You* become a boy?'

With her beautiful eyes fixed on far horizons, which she saw and we didn't, she said, 'Why not? So long as the government accepts only boys, I'll dress up in a galabia and turban and go along with you, exactly like you. Nobody's going to find out. What's the difference between boys and girls?'

We laughed, Mahjoub and I, in various ways: in scorn at her, annoyance at her, and in admiration and love.

'In your view a girl's like a boy?' Mahjoub said to her.

'Why not?'

'There's no difference?' I asked her.

'None at all,' she said.

'The very same?' Mahjoub said to her.

'Why not?'

'You and I are just the same?' I said to her.

'Except for—.'

"Except for—?' I said, egging her on.

'The nonsense bit,' she said.

'Nonsense bit yourself!' said Mahjoub, guffawing with laughter.

But she was not deterred. Suddenly she was facing us and we saw the lights of that distant horizon shining on her forehead and round her eyes. We looked at each other like persons bewitched and we said, Mahjoub and I, in a single voice, that far-off horizon becoming apparent to us as well, 'That's right, why not?'

Our voices were devoid of irony and had taken on a slight tinge of awe.

'The fact is that the classes at school aren't full,' said Mahjoub.

'And every day,' I said, 'the headmaster's out on his donkey up river and down imploring people to bring their sons along to the school.'

'And all day long I've nothing to do,' said Maryam, 'just visiting this relative and that.'

'And Maryam's clever,' said Mahjoub.

'And she wants to do it,' I said.

'And it's a pity not to,' said Maryam.

As though we were a chorus welcoming in a dawn that had begun to appear, the three of us said in one voice, 'That's right, why not?'

That forenoon, though at the time I did not know that the bond between her and me would shortly and forever be severed, she said, 'That's it, the marriage will be tonight. But I've not yet got myself ready for it.'

Mahjoub did not understand, but I realized at once what she meant.

'God willing,' I said to her, 'everything will turn out all right. Don't worry at all.'

There had been nothing wrong with her and she had been in bed for only one day: it was as though she had made up her mind suddenly to depart, as though all that happened had not happened. He was on her right and I was on her left; we alone were with her, as she wanted it. She was as beautiful as a bride; nothing wrong with her except some beads of sweat on her forehead. Her face was radiant, her eyes shining like flashes of lightning. She looked at me for an instant as though she did not know me; then, looking at Mahjoub, she said, 'But Meryoud hasn't arrived yet. How can the marriage take place when Meryoud hasn't yet returned from his travels?'

Then Mahjoub understood and burst out sobbing.

'Meryoud has arrived,' he said to her, weeping. 'Everything is ready for the wedding.'

'He's returned?' she said joyfully. 'Since when?'

'I'm Meryoud, Maryoum,' I said to her. 'Of course the contract will be concluded tonight. Everything is ready.'

She searched my face, anger showing in her eyes, and was once again as I remember her forty or more years ago.

'You're not Meryoud. You're Bakri. I'd never marry Bakri. Never. Never.'

'How can you say he's not Meryoud?' Mahjoub said to her. 'It's he himself, just arrived.'

Again she scrutinized my face.

'Are you deluded or what, Maryoum?' I said to her.

In another voice, as though she were another person, she said, 'The eyes are those of Meryoud. The nose is that of Meryoud. The voice is that of Meryoud. But you're not Meryoud. Meryoud's younger. You're not Meryoud at all. Who are you?'

She was silent for a while, then said, 'Perhaps you are Meryoud. You're Meryoud and yet not Meryoud. A person and not a person. You're not any person or any thing.' Then she wept and said, 'A pity. Meryoud is dead. And me, they're going to marry me off to Bakri. Never. It's better for me to die than marry Bakri.'

After that she dozed off and became still. We thought that we had lost her. Suddenly she woke up and there was something in her face and everything about her – and in us along with her: it was as though the lovers' howdahs had begun their departure.

'Quickly, quickly,' she said. 'The appointed time has come. The time is nigh. At last I'm ready to travel. It is best for us to say farewell now. Goodbye. Goodbye. Take care of yourselves – and the children – '

Mahjoub kissed her on the cheek, barely able to control his tears. I bent over her and kissed her forehead. She clung to me and hugged me, and I sensed in her something like a precious secret, something impossible. That perfume. That time of youth. That dream. The wheel of time had gone backwards until it stopped at a moonlit summer's night, not of this time or this earth. I heard the sound of my weeping as though someone else were letting flow the tears that had been kept imprisoned all those years. This is my portion of everything. This is my share, my inheritance. He had died before her and had left her to me, to die in my arms. Perhaps it was for this that I had returned.

She was like a bird. Mahjoub lifted her up from her bier and the light from the lanterns at the edge of the grave flared. I heard the winds of Amsheer calling to me with Maryam's tongue, 'Nothing. No one.' Carrying her, he stepped towards the grave, and I stood in his way and stretched out my arms. He looked at me for an instant and I saw his eyes growing limpid and filling with tears, then he gave her up to me. She was light as a young bird as I walked with her along a road stretching from place to place, from plain to mountain. It was not a dream. Not at all. Maryam was asleep on my shoulder. I carried her along a river's bank till the forenoon when the burning of the sun on her face woke her up. Slipping from me, she was leapt into the water. She was naked. I averted my gaze, but then I was unable to control myself and I turned my face to her. I looked and found that she was in a pool of light, and it was as though the sun's rays had deserted everything else and had clung to her body. She would dive in and then surface, disappearing at one spot and reappearing at another, laughing at me from the direction of my right, then calling me from the left. Yes. Yes. Yes. I want to drown in the pool of that light that is not of the lights of this time or of this earth. Yet I hesitated, not for more than the twinkling of an eye. In that instant the ray returned to its source, the vision went, where I knew not. I called at the top of my voice, 'Maryoum. Maryoum,' and the echo came back magnified into various voices, 'Meryoud. Meryoud.' I set off aimlessly in a desolate desert, its wind howling, its sands shifting, until I was overcome by despair and exhaustion. Then I found a talh tree, its blossom gleaming. I threw myself down by it. Suddenly I was conscious of Maryam, a little after midnight or shortly before dawn, I know not. But I do recollect a thin darkness and a light that poured out upon my face from her eyes. I drank of it but I was then consumed by thirst.

'Shall I not go with you,' I said to her, 'for I am stronger now?'

'No,' she said. 'You retrace your steps and I shall go on from here alone.'

'But I – ' I said.

She said, 'You will not be able to keep up with me, for behind this wilderness are mountains, and behind the mountains is a sea, and behind the sea is neither this nor that. The call is for me alone. You return and I'll go on.'

Then she took my head and placed it in her lap, as she rocked me and sang me a lullaby in a voice which was as soft and tenuous as ants moving on a sand-dune.

'Do not be sad, O light of my eyes, for I shall not be far away. You will see me and you will hear my voice,' she said to me.

I said and I was not I: 'Alas. Alas.'

It was then that she kissed me between the eyes and smiled with all the beauty of her face into mine, and said, 'Yes, yes, O pomegranate of my heart. If you are in need of me, then call me and I shall come.'

I said: 'Alas. Alas.'

'But,' she said, 'you must be patient and submit.'

'Then make for me a sign,' I said.

'Your sign,' she said, 'is water. Your sign is water. You will forever be looking back. Your sign is to remain wide awake to the end of time. You will see me and I shall help you as much as I can.'

'Let me go some steps with you, to see you on your way.'

'No, O apple of my heart,' she said. 'Here is the parting of the ways, and it is farewell.'

My heart was wrenched with sadness and I did not find the tears with which to cool the heat inside me, for she had robbed me of the blessing of weeping.

'Then supply me with provisions for my journey,' I said to her.

'No,' she said.

'Supply me,' I said.

'No,' she said.

'Supply me,' I said.

'No,' she said.

'Supply me,' I said.

'Alas, my beloved,' she said. 'The best of provisions is I. And it is here that I part from you. You will know no repletion, no quenching of the thirst after me. You will find no help and no deliverance. Roam where you will and take along provisions if you can, and seek deliverance – until you shall meet me when I shall give you manna and solace.'

Then she was out of reach and I heard her voice as though it was coming down from the sky and surrounding me from all directions, winds enwrapping it, winds unfolding it.

'O Meryoud. You are nothing. You are no one, Meryoud. You have chosen your grandfather and your grandfather has chosen you because the two of you are most weighty in the scales of the people of the world. And your father is greater than both of you in the scales of Justice. He loved without growing weary, he gave without hope of any reward, and he sipped as a bird sips, and he lived as though continually about to travel, and he departed in a hurry. He dreamt the dreams of the meek, and he partook of the provisions of the poor; he was tempted by glory but he restrained himself, and when life called him – when life called him – '

I said yes. I said yes. I said yes. But the way back was harder because I had forgotten.

NOTES TO
BOOKS ONE & TWO

BOOK ONE

1. He is dead, as is recounted in *Season of Migration to the North*.
2. The literal meaning of the nickname is someone who gives supper to girls who would otherwise go to sleep on empty stomachs, i.e. someone generous and chivalrous.
3. The opening and closing words of the Fatiha, the equivalent in Islam of the Lord's Prayer.
4. Title given to the Caliph.
5. The night in the month of Ramadan in which the Koran was revealed. It is held to be an especially auspicious night for having prayers answered.
6. Described in the short story *A Handful of Dates*.
7. The subject of the novel *The Wedding of Zein*.
8. A person hired to recite panegyric poetry at weddings and other ceremonies.
9. A well-known hero of ancient times.
10. Village headman.
11. Hasan Crocodile.
12. God-help-us son of Jabr and Dar.
13. Bekheit Father-of-Girls.
14. Suleiman Nabag-eating.
15. Slave-of-the-Lord son of Cupboard-key.
16. The Uncoverer son of God's mercy.
17. The son of Haleema, who is his mother, while normally the father's name is used.
18. There is no such chapter in the Koran. These are the names of letters to be found at the beginning of several of its chapters.
19. A Coptic month, proverbially the coldest in winter.
20. A Koranic reference.
21. In a verse in the Koran it is said that God is nearer to one than his jugular vein.
22. The set prayer ends with these words.
23. A small area of cultivated land.
24. The first words of one of the Prophet's sayings.
25. Room in which guests are received.

26. The two statements uttered by the grandfather and Wad Haleema make up the doctrinal formula of faith in Islam.
27. Someone wearing Western dress and working in an office.
28. As told in the short story *The Doum Tree of Wad Hamid*.
29. The names of Arabic letters to be found at the beginning of certain chapters in the Koran.
30. A form of greeting used to Christians and Jews.
31. 'War' in Farsi.
32. The words mean 'May God be with us'; it is an exclamation normally used only by women.
33. A reference from the Koran.
34. i.e. the Light of the House.
35. A feddan is approximately one acre.
36. A well-known folk hero.

BOOK TWO

1. i.e. Happy Pilgrim, Asha 'l-Baytat's first name is Sa'eed, which means 'happy'. Having performed the pilgrimage, he may use the title 'hajj' (pilgrim), thus becoming 'happy pilgrim'.
2. Bilal was an Abyssinian slave whom the Prophet made Islam's first muezzin.
3. i.e. on the Day of Judgement. The words refer to a verse in the Koran.
4. A Sufi term meaning spiritual leader.
5. i.e. 'Rawwas' in Arabic.
6. A head tax imposed on non-Moslems in a Moslem state.
7. i.e. someone descended from the Prophet.
8. The angel who will sound the trumpet on the Day of Resurrection.
9. The angel who bestows good things on men.
10. The angel of death.
11. The words and actions of the Prophet.
12. Their destruction is mentioned in the Koran.
13. The final words of the Fatiha, the equivalent of the Lord's Prayer.
14. These names are all from the same root letters as that of Mohammed, the Prophet.
15. A pet form of Maryam.
16. It is the practice among Moslems to add the words 'may the blessings and peace be upon him' after mention of the Prophet.